ANCA CRISTOFOVICI

ninebark

ISBN 978-0-9791320-3-2

Cover & Interior Design: Lou Robinson

ninebark
Rome, GA & Salt Lake City, UT
http://www.ninebarkpress.org/

Ninebark Press is sponsored by the Rome Area Council for the
Arts. Tax-deductible contributions designated for Ninebark Press
may be addressed to Ninebark Press/RACA, 3 Central Plaza, Suite
359, Rome, GA 30161

Contents

On the Other Side

Circles of leaves and dust rise toward a horizon of storm. With hurried steps we make our way through the crowd. Stela takes my hand in hers, then suddenly drops it, slows her pace, and, barely reaching my bony shoulder, urges me forward.

Say *pardon*, she says in a low voice, *par-don*, as she used to prompt me when I was her child and had no doubt that Mother knew the right thing to do. Was this still true? Who knows? We have no time for questions. On the other side of the street, two men in gray suits are waiting for us, pretending to provide protection. Their presence constricts my margin of action. Given the circumstances, all I can do is keep an eye on Stela. She is here now, and clarifying whatever might be worth clarifying isn't going to change anything, nor bring us any farther than that.

On the other side, two gigantic zebras come into sight. They trot alongside a row of sumptuous buildings. Slender but firm, their hips swing with a rhythm they alone seem to master. Through the curtain of dust, their gait stupefies us, and as they move onward, the stripes on their backs dissolve in the murky air. At the corner of the street, in a perfectly orchestrated choreography, the zebras pass three ostriches walking from the opposite direction, as colossal as they are, as momentous. The coat of feathers covering their bodies, ashy in color and consistency, could be blown away any minute by a gust of wind.

Uncannily elegant, their pace is firm.

Their ancestral, reptile heads make me uncomfortable.

The heat seems suddenly too heavy to bear. We lack space. My throat packed with dust, I turn to check if Mother's still there and take her hand in mine, by now about the same size as hers. A bird slashes the air above our heads. Stela takes its harsh wailing as a signal of our impending displacement from what she calls the "Jungle Zone" to the "Menagerie Zone." In light of her experience, she insists, the displacement risks becoming systematic and chaotic. *And*—not *or*—chaotic, she points out. This odd idea seems to flow from what she said earlier: that, since we are related, our separation was mandatory to prevent the dissemination of the likes of us in space.

Slowly, I remove my hand from hers to sketch out the options we have with naïve gestures intended to convince Mother that I'm able to protect her. It's a matter of security (undoubtedly a pun to her), I argue, and, in spite of my inappropriate, insistent words, I'm trying to be as affectionate and reassuring as I can. For all that, my arguments clash with her unequivocal smile.

As we turn our eyes from that scene in slow motion, the horizon has grown into a maze of branches. Their swinging overwhelms us. The sky is neither luminous nor dark. Still, some formless substance, more like a blinding light, presses on our eyelids. It seems to come from a source other than the sun: a magnifying glass, or the goggled eye of a commanding bird.

In the middle of its crystalline lens, we are misty figures.

Given the situation (patterns of space, atmosphere, geometry of humors), all I can to do for now is keep looking after Stela.

STELA'S RETURN

{1}

Green

Her eyes were still a tender green but, as she glanced over the dull platform, they transformed into rare shades.

She was being returned by a government official who appeared unwilling to leave her solely in my care. He was in charge of helping us out, he said: to find us an apartment, to assist her in settling in, to reassure us that from now on everything was going to be as it should. B. K. was not unattractive. Alert. Attentive. Anxious to see us safe. The tanned, lizard skin of his face added to his appeal as it did to his bossy air. When I saw them emerge from the train—he in front, holding her hand obligingly, she, hardly brushing the steps—it was eight o'clock in the morning, in the middle of summer. The heat was already livening up. I couldn't help being tired.

Her body was thin. A body of air: watchful, reserved.

Stela stepping off the train in slow motion, drifting out of sleep or some other inert state unfit for the situation. A woman still attached to some remote landscape, in no haste to reach my comforting arms haunted by her absence.

It was hard to tell if her features had been firmed or rather blurred by the spaces she had passed through. Her listless pace in contrast to her startled gaze, her indifference to words, and a disregard for me that I soon experienced in the most unexpected ways only added to the surprise and confusion I felt at her sudden appearance, then at her reticence, which—apart from a few moments—she maintained throughout her brief return from her long journey.

Yet what could I expect? She must have been fifty-five by then, and I thirty-five. Still, in spite of this gap, we looked about the same age.

Mother had been declared dead twenty years ago to the day.

If truth be told, from the onset, that declaration had seemed to me inaccurate, dubious, fake. I was certainly the only one to stand up against it, against the very particulars that had brought the event to my knowledge upon my return from a dancing tour in a neighboring country, one month after Stela's disappearance. The facts of her death had reached me through the voice of an acquaintance of hers when I was trying to spot Mother in a crowd dressed in black meeting me at the train station. The woman's lozenge-shaped earrings dangled languidly in the ruthless heat of early August. As she projected her dismaying words in my direction, a short man, half-hidden behind her heavy body, moved his hands in a pantomime that made her pathetic phrases redundant, the intervention of both of them in my life suspect, lacking in elegance or diplomacy.

No other memory attached these people to my life, except for the vague detail that both the husband and his wife—who I insist was not a close friend of Mother's, though they had once worked together at a hospital in our city—had at some point been employed at our country's embassy in Cuba. When Mother spoke about the man's job—first here, then there—she called it "The Cypher," a word I associated with some game that produced an unpleasant, nauseating effect reinforced by their acting as unexpected messengers of Stela's death.

Two snails. Two snail flesh faces, their individual features concealed by a slimy film of sweat. Do they eat snails in Cuba? Had the man been deciphering snail language there? Had he left traces for others to efface? In whose name were they passing this incongruous message about Mother to me?

A lump of disgust throbbed in my throat. I couldn't bear snails even if I were to starve. The shabby mise en scène of their overdone distress concerning Mother's death, their garish compassion with regard to my humble self made me bluntly sick.

I slammed the door in everyone's face.

Blue & Green Motifs

A shadow of doubt hovered over Stela's disappearance despite the circumstances of her death, which the couple revealed to me down to the minutest detail, with material evidence, yet in a curious order that I can barely remember.

If we stick to facts, there was a car. A red car, they told me, a trendy brand almost unknown in our small country or in the surrounding region, driven by a man whose identity had not yet, and has never, been disclosed. A foreigner undoubtedly, and, naturally, ominous. Driving far above the speed limit. Fast enough to mow down a woman, her eyes briefly turned from the road by a sudden remembrance.

A broken cheekbone. On the right side.

Then, shortly after sunrise, around six o'clock: a commotion. Or its belated manifestation.

A newspaper clipping. A minor news item.

Pictures from the funeral were produced to confirm details given to me by the two I persist in calling "the cypher friends," since the information they gave me was beyond my grasp.

They were even so considerate as to hand me the dress she had been wearing that day they called "the day of the accident." Washed and ironed. A batiste summer dress. Blue and green motifs touched here and there by brown auras or accidents, the kind that blood leaves when it has, or has nearly, dried.

The exact tone of blue that matches a certain tone of green.

{*3*}

Plots

In spite of these irrefutable proofs, she was here now. Twenty years later. B. K. was doing his best to find us a place to settle. When I saw the places he was looking for, fear supplanted my intuition about her being tied to him in some arcane way. Sumptuous buildings with heavy gates, unending, high-ceilinged corridors coated with mirrors, bleak vestibules separated from vast rooms by leather-covered double doors that might have absorbed sounds of all kinds—sighs, murmurs, moans of despair, who knows what? Buildings deprived of their proper inhabitants. Interiors more like dubious offices. In each of them we were to spend a few days, "a trial period," he called it. Something definitely beyond my grasp was going on, and, as Stela's eyes were telling me, it was beyond hers, as well.

These places in no way suited Mother's taste and they suited mine even less. It was hard for me to understand why she didn't say a word, hard for me to break the ice, to ask her questions about where she was returning from. What kind of questions should they be? About geography? Climate? Customs of the locals? Who was who? Provide a few examples, Mother! I needed some kind of evidence other than that summer dress with the blue and green motifs, the accidents of brown, something other than the newspaper clipping.

Her skirt swinging with the graceful rhythm of her steps, she walks over heaps of debris to reach something.

Between us words were scarce. Mother and I were almost never alone. Every day, apartment visits and other events related to moving from here to there were taking place according to a chaotic scheme that B. K. proudly called "the plan." And because nothing seemed to meet B. K.'s expectations, we got up and got on the road again every morning, following his plan. If my first glimpse of him had been anything but dour, now there were certainly reasons for circumspection. Little by little, my hope of sharing a roof with Stela for a while turned vain. Obviously, something was making (forcing?) Mother to settle in with B. K. or to spend a period of purification in these outlandish apartments or offices where he wanted to put us up. Doubt was creeping into my already laconic relationship with Mother. Where, after all, was I supposed to be in the picture? For twenty years I had made my life without her even as I kept picturing how she would, someday, return. But I never thought about what would become of me if one of the versions of that scenario materialized.

We spent our time moving from one zone to another, as if we were still being shadowed, alternating means of transportation: local trains and cars, buses and tramways, and in between, pursuing our silent march. It was not so much the distance between one zone and another that upset me, or even that we were still unable to settle anywhere, since, after Stela's departure, I had attached myself to not belonging. No, it was not distance that troubled me, but rather the change in directions, abrupt, chaotic changes, again and again, guided by nothing more than vague details concerning our potential destination.

In these unpropitious circumstances, she eventually started talking, in bits and pieces, about her *kidnapping*. Her first words sounded like her mind was on the wrong track. Then I thought of Luca, his studio, his canvases, their pungent odor. When I slammed the door in everyone's face, he had opened his. Luca and his camera. Confiscated. Photographs of buildings in the neighborhood. Bleak buildings. Ordinary. Black-and-white film. Pernicious to the good of all.

It was Luca who first spoke the word, naming what I was trying to tell him about my version of Mother's disappearance. I liked that word I'd never heard before, its comforting sound. Like a kid's nap. That's how much you can trust words. Luca shifted the stress. But that was in another country, he said. Such things happened outside our perimeter in those "years of lead." Besides, she wasn't anyone. Outstanding, he added. No matter, I kept thinking, there was still the possibility that….

Since the cypher friends' dubious report, had I not thought of her being in another country? Having trespassed? Or having been taken out of the country thanks to someone's intervention? Certainly, once she was out of the area under surveillance, she must have hesitated to get in touch with me so as not to aggravate my situation. No doubt, a time would come when she would find the means to take me out of the country. Such things happened, here and there. One heard about them, now and then. Whispers, rumors. I had to keep hoping. Luca's equivocations aside, I dared to think she had escaped being a camouflaged hostage as we all were (most of us), in that place, at that time.

.

Luca did share my doubts regarding the official cause of Mother's disappearance, yet he seemed to harbor another belief than the one I had formed early on, namely that she had defected to some unknown destination and temporarily abandoned me only to come to my rescue later, whenever that turned out to be possible. Was he holding anything back from me? Were his hints intended to hide or rather to reveal a decisive detail that would put us on the right track to find out how and why exactly Stela had disappeared? If our doubts were certain, no matter how hard we tried to make up a better version than her death, we never came close to a coherent alternative to Mother's fatal accident.

Luca saying: "Look at this picture, Cora dear."

"What picture?"

It was a faded photograph, crumpled as if someone had wanted to do away with it. The photo had been taken in the summer known as the summer "of the accident."

"It's not her, Luca."

"I don't mean Stela, I mean you. Look at the man."

"What man?"

"The man in the photo, there, behind you, leaning on the fence, narrowing his eyes at you from under the slanting brim of his hat."

"It's not about him, the photo. Who cares? He's just a passerby."

"A passerby? No other lead?"

Details without tenor: a washed-out gray oversized suit (obsolete cut, covered buttons), hat brim at a dubious angle. Not the tourist type, plainly. A passerby, one of many hanging around the streets of the city, reading papers in a corner or taking shelter in a phone booth. Clumsy, affecting an absent air along the dusty sidewalks. Trained to watch, as they all were, but rather looking like bit players in a bad movie. Luca made a point about the man staring at me and, eventually, about the possibility of his shadowing me as I was putting up an awkward smile for the camera's sake.

"Shadowing me? What for?"

"I'm only telling you about things that happen," Luca said.

He smelled of verbena. His skin was soft. I had no one else willing to help.

While I was imagining Stela abroad, Luca favored the local plot and was keen on such details as inconspicuous, clumsy men in faded summer photos. Soon I ran short of details for my own version, but now, as Stela and I walked in a derelict landscape, the little man in the picture came back to my mind. He looked, if I remembered well, not unlike the men on B. K.'s staff: effaced, solicitous, peculiarly curious. Who knows? They all looked so much the same.

But back then, what did I know? Everybody thought there was no need I know more. An aura of mystery and exception had always surrounded Mother, and the nebulous details of her disappearance only added to that. Everybody seemed to think there was no need to talk. No need to talk about Stela.

Even Luca wouldn't bring me farther into his story.

Missing links, I thought.

Too many.

Turning them over and over in my mind *to reach something that is no more than a breach now.*

{4}

Stela with Flowers

Some days before the call from the government official's secretary notifying me of Stela's arrival and soliciting my presence at the Main Station of our small capital on August eighth at eight o'clock in the morning "to welcome your mother" (metallic voice, starched articulations laying the words bare):

Stela in the front yard of our city house.

Stela passing through a bright gallery: flowering tobacco or queens-of-the-night: white, star-shaped, hypnotic.

Datura enhancing the fragrance that made us one in the night.

Cosmos in lavender pink, violet, and white hues.

Cornflower in blue spots.

Wild chamomile.

Stela's lips forming imperfect circles, spelling out a silent code of colors in the strategies of survival.

Summer seems without end as I come near her and she ignores my presence, or is unable to notice it.

She moves a slow hand, picks a white flower, sticks it in her hair. Brown is her hair, and as it spreads on her shoulders it turns red, thick, viscid, drips along her arm, down her index finger pointing to the mailbox.

The mailbox is by the entrance gate, made of wood and shaky.

The postman has a rusted bicycle and a blue, washed-out uniform. He's already gone. He comes back.

"Peek-a-boo," he shrieks. "How's your grandfather's au-to-mo-bile, by the way? We've got a nice one, don't we, from the old times."

He says, "Your dog barks at me."

"Here's a piece of bread for your dog," he says. "Foreign brand, that car. Stubborn man, he was. *Kistibur!*"

"What?"

"You, granddaughter of a *kistibur*. Unhealthy origins. To the roots. And, say smarty, how many languages does that mom of yours speak? Feeding you with them too, smarty, ain't she?"

"We are honest people, sir."

"Sir!" he grins. "We've finished them off, those sirs! But they've got offspring like you, smarty. Too many languages. Foreign, like that car. You get letters from abroad, don't I know about that. Yeah! You think yourselves clever, ed-u-ca-ted! Phew!"

The blood dripping from Mother's index finger has grown into a pool at her feet. Soon it reaches my toes. It's lukewarm, soothing.

"No good languages. Not in the register. Not allowed."

"What register, sir? Don't you see my mother's bleeding to death?"

"Who cares! I'm a nice guy no matter what you think, ready to lend a helping hand. Here's bread for your dog."

"Don't you touch my dog," I shout, "or Mother will kill you."

"Phew!"

His sneering laughter lags behind him, and a thick odor of sweat with it.

Mother keeps stroking the dog with her unhurt hand. She pours milk into a bowl but he won't have it. He gulps from the red pool instead. Milk isn't good against poison, I suddenly remember, but she seems not to. The dog must know there's something wrong with Mother but doesn't want to upset her, or wants to help her as he can. With his pale tongue he clears up the pool at her feet.

Perhaps she too does what she can under the circumstances.

On the hand that pours the milk into the dog's bowl, Mother wears the unsold ring. She's fed me on the others. That's one thing the postman doesn't know about—how Grandmother had sold all they had, rings, coins, and necklaces, on the black market to feed me—or he just doesn't care about that because there is already enough proof against us.

The pile of letters overwhelms the box hanging on the lattice gate *with nothing behind, like a stage set with a wall in ruins through the gaps of which one can see the sky.*

It's shortly before sunrise. The sky has turned a washy blue. One of the letters drops to the ground. I pick it up. My hands are damp. The clumsy handwriting in copying pencil turns purple and blurred where my fingers touch it. The name of the addressee is smeared. My fingers are blotted. Then, they start bleeding, like Mother's.

Heavy drops the air upon my shoulders.

Rough, dense, irremediable.

I tear the envelope open. Flat on the ground, the dog looks up at me. His coat is short, smooth, the color of sand. His tongue is dry.

```
Acknowledge hereby the death of S. A. You
are authorized to reclaim her body and
personal effects at the police station,
District No.1. A proof of kinship will be
requested.
```

I, daughter of Stela, inheritor of tender green—proof of kinship at best.

The queens-of-the-night fading in the back of the yard carry Stela's shadow.
That can't be so.
She *is* dead.
Mother, I mutter, *cannot die twice.*

{5}

Rescuing Mother

The huge apartments B. K. made us visit were so unlike our home or any other space I have lived in. It was not their overwhelming size that made them inhospitable but rather their ugliness, an offending distortion of harmony that repelled words spoken at normal pitch, considerate gestures, trust. Something menacing emanated from their drab walls, something massive and anarchic to boot, bearing potentially negative—if not irremediable—consequences for our corporeal integrity were Stela and I to live there.

One of those places in particular, a former mansion in the capital's residential zone, seemed to attract B. K.'s favor. Two sturdy columns of indeterminate style protected its entrance. Ivy hid their volume. The shape of the house itself was less repulsive than the shadow of inappropriate use, of violence and stupidity, of groundless hate.

A stifling place, stale, suffused with an accumulation of gross detail that offended the eye. The interior reeked of brutality, humiliation, neglect. A sad pattern of nondescript color concealed layers of paint on the walls. They resonated with voices calling out for help and solid silence in response to them. I could not imagine Mother waking up with her eyes caught in such a contrived fabric. But, I conceded, there may have been reasons for B. K.'s insisting that we live there (or for Mother accepting such a proposition) that escaped me.

B. K. showed me to the double door upholstered with ersatz leather, mumbling that he and Mother had things to discuss. This smelled of conspiracy. Outside, with a muffled battering of wings throbbing in my eardrums, I realized that I might never see Stela again. That she might disappear once more.

I had to get her out of danger.

How could I do so with nothing at hand? Rescue Mother? My pockets were empty. How could I prevent Stela from making a decision that might aggravate the already odd circumstances of our reunion? Could I send her a warning? Something casual, not necessarily words? A code, say, that Stela alone could make sense of. As precarious as my means were, I had to save Mother from disappearing again, perhaps forever.

After all, no one here had knowledge of her return, except for me, B. K., and his staff.

Who but I would care about the color of her eyes?

From a corner of the garden, I could make out B. K.'s left shoulder in the window. A triangle of his navy blue suit, half a circle of the vaguely white collar of his shirt, half of his grayish hair. That was less than a third of his body cropped in the window frame, and more than what I could take of B. K. for the time being.

But could he care less? Deeply rooted in his immediate reality, with his left arm now placed in a right angle on the windowsill, he must have been projecting his predictable rhetoric at Mother to persuade her that this was the kind of home we needed.

He slashed the air with ample gestures, while the angle of his left arm got smaller and smaller, slowly passing out of my view. A more or less white surface then took B. K.'s place in the window frame, or it might have been a trick of my tired eyes.

In the space of an instant, Mother's head moved across the window, drew a curve from left to right, as if grabbed by some device out of view. No doubt, she had no way of seeing me crouching there in the garden, my woman's chin on my kid's knees. But I had to persist—one has to—in saving Mother's life (unless she was there to save mine).

With my nails, I sketched a bird's body on the scorched soil. Then an ectoplasm of sorts sprouting from its beak. And inside, with my nails, I scratched:

try out a lie!

But I knew Mother wouldn't do that. I wiped the words away with the back of my hand. Then I wrote:

stand firm!

A gust of wind blurred the letters and the awkward bird's body with them. I looked back at the now empty window and, hitting the ground with my fists, blew a soft ball of breath:

Mutterlicht

It was something only Mother would understand.

As she walked down the front stairs of that dreadful house, I heard her say, with a self-possessed tone I'd never noticed before, in a voice I could hardly remember:

"Thank you!"

And then:

"It is not within our means."

In spite of whatever she owed B. K., she was, after all, putting some trust in me. If to my mind what she said made little sense,

I knew she had uttered the words she had to in a life-threatening situation.

Mother always did.

Or used to.

We passed under the gate, she and I.

Stela carried a white cat in her arms.

It was all she could do, under the circumstances.

{6}

Stela and I in the Botanic Garden

What I first learned about her detention—from the bits she gave out, in her slow, obsolete idiom as we moved from one zone to another—was that she had, in fact, not been in absolute confinement. They had granted her the comforts of a small room, *after a while*. On her apathetic lips, the phrase sounded suspect, with that indefinite indication of time, like a scrap of paper swept up by the wind. Of what had happened in the early days, she wasn't saying a word.

Though brought to live in a confined zone, which was not exactly a prison, she had the essentials, Stela insisted, as we leaned on the iron fence of an abandoned square to rest; she even had a bit of pocket money and, in order to make good use of her free time without breaking the rules, permission to borrow books from the local library. There were, no doubt, books she had no access to because they were unavailable, but she read everything that *was* available so she could try to figure out what was going on in the world.

I pointed out that, in any event, the picture of the world she would likely have made there—remote as the world was to her at the time, wherever she was—had every chance of turning out partial, if not faked.

She looked down, making small loops in the sand with the point of her shoe. But, to me, that didn't count as information.

My words rose above her head, above the trees and roofs, a ventriloquist's voice she had never heard before—alien even to me. I jumped on my perch, telling her, now that she was here, everything I knew about life and, most of all, about my own life, which she seemed to have ignored.

"Yes,"

she replied humbly, with no reaction against my anger

"Yes, no doubt, but—

"I was there—and that's the way it was."

"*The way it was*, and you did nothing to leave the place. You stayed there and watched your life pass, with nothing to say. Yes, not too much lip, don't I know about that?"

My stock phrases thrown at her evasions did not seem to touch her. They turned against me instead, and they hurt. I had not intended to upset Mother. By no means. But her words made no sense to my impatient mind. Her slow gestures, her disinterest in my life exasperated me. She had nothing else to say, no question about what had happened to me in her absence, or to her mother, to the house, to whatever she'd left behind twenty years before.

Where did I fit in the picture? After so many years among strangers, I, too, had become a stranger to her. She wasn't able to love me anymore! Perhaps she had never loved me. I couldn't help provoking her. My misplaced tone, my ill-fitting words stormed at Mother all at once without the slightest intention of hurting her. But I couldn't help it: she seemed now someone other than the woman I had been talking to all these years—in my mind, or in letters without a destination—yes, quite another person, even if her features had remained so surprisingly unaltered. Not only wasn't she saying much about her long journey, or whatever it was that took her away, but she also didn't seem to want to know anything about mine.

Or maybe she was just tired.

Yes. I must have thought of that as she descended the train's steps that first day back. Fatigue. She wore it like a tightly woven net over her face, down her body. It slowed her pace. Her figure had not been diminished by time, but rather blurred, and it became obvious that she could hardly follow my eager steps, much less my questions. Still, Mother's slowness was difficult to understand (and to accept), her lethargic step unnerving. *Interstice* came to my mind, and I suddenly wondered what had happened to the blood in her veins.

But that was no time for explanations. For now, she just needed to take a rest.

B. K. and his staff busied themselves with their meetings. He appointed two men in petrol blue suits to protect us. The two young men, uncomfortable in their disguise and somewhat puzzled by our indifference to them, agreed to a breach in the plan so long as we stayed within the zone. I dragged Mother to the Botanic Garden, the two men lagging behind, stopping by the gate to light their damp cigarettes. It was a break they could enjoy as well.

We sat down on a bench. A stone bench. Someone had notched a name on its back. It said: *Daniel, good companion.*

At our feet, fidgety crows picked at whatever they found: crumbs, cigarette butts, greasy paper.

"Intelligent animals," Mother said. "Look how they hop around after their bits of food. Look at the one over there softening a dry crumb in a puddle. Sometimes, you know, sometimes I think they are laughing at us."

We watched people pass, Stela and I, for a while. Their weary steps around us stirred the path's dry, scarred soil, transforming it into golden dust above our heads. In the distance, the garden's green space dissolved into an outburst of clear water. So much clear and green water.

A house on a lake loomed in the distance. Small and tidy. Maybe the lake keeper's, with its own garden in front. A good place to live. The air smelled of lake and water weeds, of wild lilies.

My shoulder brushed hers. We both contemplated the lake, then the small garden.

An errant bird tried out a branch, then drifted to the ground. Lead gray, its body weighed down by pain.

"I had a radio . . ." I heard her say out of the blue, her lagging syllables at last carrying a sentence to its end, though I remained indifferent to what I took to be a detail of no importance.

" . . . buzzing, whirring, purring. Far into the night, no more local news, no more fanfares, just voices, zigzagging tones, languages in great numbers, many of them unknown (and so much the better). With a deft turn of the switch, that I had all the time in the world to practice, I made them melt into each other. Like chocolate into milk or, who knows, egg yolks into creamed butter and sugar. Round, harsh, soft, or puffy syllables. I added them up as I lay there, trying to figure things out.

"As the sounds faded slowly away, sleep came by.

"Night after night they kept me going, those voices.

"A night's sound sleep was a better day's life.

"And down there in my chest, the syllables throbbed, tick-tacked.

"Once, a pitch so high, like sound rising over a huge obstacle, woke me up. Like that dog over there—there—trying to find his way over that hedge. Too high that voice for a human voice. Too far away. Then, a flat announcement followed: ee-ma-su-mac. What was I to make of it?

"My own voice, I couldn't raise it. But sense or no sense, I kept them there, down in my chest, the other voices. Cracking, pattering, broken sounds.

"An accident? Countless. Small. Insidious. Invisible. Adding up.

"Ether. Not the smell of ether, but its effect.

"A catastrophe? Who said so? No. Nothing. I tell you, Cora, my one and only child: *nothing.*

"And, as time passes, the shock you expect still fails to happen. There is no disaster."

She produced a blunt pencil from her left pocket and a folded piece of tissue paper from the other. With the back of her hand, she smoothed out the paper and let the pencil find its way. I noticed she no longer wore the only ring she had been left with, and then I remembered it was now on my finger.

A map of dusty roads is what she drew. Or was it a disposition of streams, rivulets? A trellis of wire? Blood came to mind.

"Interstice?" I tried.

"You see!"

In spite of the fatigue, her eyes, the color of lemon sprouts now, glimmered with anticipation.

"A lattice of veins and nerves," I proceeded, "and, in between, a small crack, an empty space. Is that so?"

Details slowly came back to me from the days when she sketched the insides of bodies on crisp drafting paper to show me what made them work.

"See, you are getting to it! That's where it happens, the accident. Right there. Somewhere in the body tissue. The pain sneaks in there, and then it stays. And you keep it there as well as you can."

"What, the pain?"

"Some bundle, what: shreds, odds and ends, you know, what's left of you. You keep to it."

The pencil carried on sketching a pair of tears, or a downside drop falling on or clashing with an upside drop, something that didn't look like a muscle or a vein.

"Remember synapse?" she said. "So many of them, gaps or junctions—as your luck or genes run—between somewhere and somewhere else."

And then the pencil produced an outburst of thin pulsating lines, red and orange and blue, something like a firework inside, or synapses firing, and I sketched a question:

"It—?"

"—hurts? It can't hurt— if you have to go on."

She folded the paper with care and put it back in her pocket, as if she had accomplished something important. Then, turning her eyes away from me to follow the dog, now running on the other side of the lake, she carried on:

"The eye travels fast—who can catch sight of it traveling?

"Fold up your tear. Hang it round your neck. I have no ring left.

"The accident, as you said they called it, leaves a dummy behind: your body, plain, numb, nothing spectacular. Tears are for bystanders. And you aren't one, my dear.

"It is—how to say?—like passing away with no theatrical gesticulation.

"There's breath. And then there isn't.

"But when breath goes on, you have to keep up with it.

"The mind goes its own way. The body stays numb before you make up your mind to go on, get back in touch with your bones and flesh, tame them. From moment to moment. You wash your face. Parcel out provisions. Try the good side to sleep on. The dreams not to dream. What to say and what not to say. What not to say, above all. A protocol of moves and forms of attention that keeps you going from moment to moment. Yes, against that numbness, day in, day out.

"You dig into empty pockets, try to recall, then to forget. For whatever comes back brings along fear. Fear to hope or fear to miss. Fear that the pitch of that voice reminding you of something forgotten will someday drop off and, not long after it died out, there'll be no more to hold on to. Nothing but yourself.

"In the absence of memory you hold on to that body. Befriend it.

"Come along, you say, even as you can't piece it together.

"Crumbled, scattered, wasted: come along! Get over that hedge!

"And some pink plastic glove pushes you on—you move, you drift, you step out, if you have the chance to.

"If words are what you need, I can make this solemn declaration: I, Stela, your mother, was no one—there. That's who I was. 'The kidnapped,' or so they called me, mockingly. Neither myself nor some other. For the rest, you do as you can, invent yourself—for as long as you can.

"Surviving is no virtue. It is an act of love.

"This is our predicament, my child, but all the weight lies on your shoulders now, and there is nothing much I can do to help. But you'll find a way to carry on, I know you will. You'll make do with what's left.

"And then, what else? Yes, you want to know more. Don't I understand? But whatever I might say isn't bringing us anywhere, is it?

"Look over there. See that bird? It's come a long way.

"Birds I missed. And in dreams, the white cat was lost when there was nothing more to lose. A crane. That's what you call it?

"No, it's not gray. It's bluish silver with a thin white collar. It hasn't moved an inch since we sat down here. Not an inch. I don't think he is suffering. He's just taking a rest."

Within sleep, a leg tucked to his chest. All feather and muscle.

{7}

Beyond Suspicion

Guardians in faded brown uniforms ran up and down the garden's alleys whistling closing time. We went out by the main gate and got on the tram. The two men from B. K.'s staff took the front seats. We found seats in the back, Stela and I. The apathetic passengers sitting and standing in between them and us didn't seem to mind what we were talking about, or they pretended not to care. Some must have had good reasons.

I brought Stela back to her story, where she had left it in the Botanic Garden, and also took the opportunity to hint at how things looked from my side: her sudden disappearance, my doubts about the accident, the alternative I had imagined, namely, her defection—which was indeed plausible given the circumstances of our lives at the time, in spite of Luca's skepticism—then my astonishment following her return.

Why might she have been abducted, I asked? She silenced all my attempts to sort things out, for a while. Then she pointed out, in passing, that there are other words for what happened, depending on geography. But, after all, does the word really matter?

The tram ran lazily along its rails. We passed a block of buildings with bleached blinds. We took a sluggish turn. Stela combed
her hair with her fingers and spoke a name: *Jo-han-nes.* It was a
familiar name, and to hear it from her gave me a start. Johannes,
my trustworthy friend.

"There was a rumor, a rumor that Johannes had denounced
me to the authorities. Or—how to say?—that he, or his wife,
dropped a word to someone casually when, dismissed from their
jobs at our embassy in Cuba, they were given more modest tasks
here. They must have done it for money, I believe, medicine, traveling papers, or something else they were yearning for."

"That—is—out—of—the—question, Mother!"

As I brought my own sentence to its end, the discordance in
time struck me. One more misunderstanding in the story of Stela's departure and her subsequent return. For even if Johannes
was not a common name in our land, she must have been speaking about someone else. How could she know the Johannes I
knew, since I had met him after she died? That is, after she passed
from sight. Be that as it may, by what means could she have heard
there—wherever she was—that incongruous rumor?

Or was it here, after her return, that some well-meaning party
had, in all discretion, provided her that precious information to
help her cope with what had happened? Or help us make sense of
it, if there was any to be made.

The rails of the wobbly tram stopped in front of that day's residence. We were about to get off when I reached for my ticket in
the right-hand pocket of my jacket, to throw it in the garbage can
as Mother used to insist I should. I found instead a large handkerchief, a man's, with dark brown edges and a coin bound in a

knot at one of its corners. This was definitely not my coat. One of B. K.'s men had already jumped off the tram and was pacing up and down the cobblestone sidewalk. With one leg on the step of the tram, the other on the cobblestones, I took off the jacket and bowled it toward him, advising his friend to pinch him so he could catch it.

It was of vital importance for me, and for Mother, to remain beyond suspicion.

{8}

Whodunit?

Mother's insistence on the first name of her alleged rat, the familiarity with which she referred to him, not to mention a certain understanding she seemed to show for his gesture, or human nature, in general, made me reconsider Stela's acquaintances, those I still remembered, even vaguely, and, above all, those I had grim memories of, such as, for instance, "the cypher friends," who were so closely associated with what I knew of Mother's accident. Since their ill-omened intervention in my life, I had lost track of them, though they might not have lost track of me. Had I maintained some contact with them, be it only for the sake of form, they might have revealed more information about Mother's disappearance, and maybe that would have helped me dissipate some of my doubts about the story they presented to me. Or, who knows, trained to comply with instructions they received, they might have helped me in other ways.

In any case, something told me, as I waited for Mother to get off the tram, that when she spoke about Johannes, she might have been referring to the man cyphering useless information in some gloomy office at the embassy in Cuba, treating himself to a banana or a soda once in a while. Mother, I recalled now, knew his wife from the hospital where they both worked, before they were promoted to that office abroad, and after. Yes, hadn't I glimpsed the woman when Mother took me with her to the hospital on an off-school day, when Grandmother was too busy to take care of me?

The woman worked at the reception office and thought well of Mother, I recalled, considered her to be the type who was difficult to approach on certain topics but she also must have had knowledge of the vulnerable position Stela was in. She may even have had a hint of esteem for her dignity, I suppose, as much as it was within her mental or emotional capacities.

In any case, it remained to be determined if the rumor of this man's calamitous intervention in Mother's life proved to be true, and if so, whether it was B. K. who had slipped that information into Mother's ostensibly accepting ear, in which case he, too, was likely part of the same network of cypher friends. Obviously, finding an answer to these questions—one being the corollary of the other—risked deepening my suspicions about Stela's potential complicity in dealing with that kind of people and my doubts as to her integrity. But how could I suspect Mother?

Under such circumstances, Grandmother's words came to mind: "We are honest people."

Given how our lives drifted apart, whatever she meant by being honest was not going to clear up my confusion, unless her words implied that the paths of honest people must be littered with trials of all kinds. But that sounds rather moralizing and I wouldn't risk rushed conclusions.

Everyone does as they can.

Unfolding Possibilities

With good reason, some would like to know—if, from the start, I doubted the accident story—why I didn't investigate and assess its dependability. But what doors could anyone of my age knock at, could anyone of any age for that matter, to find out the truth? And, all things considered, what kind of truth could I uncover?

Let's say that, defying all rules and instructions, by chance or whatever means were available to me at the time, I did manage to find the right door to knock at because my determination matched that of the door's guardians. All such guardians would certainly have done everything in their power to dissuade me, wouldn't they? But there was also the possibility that these people, or their superiors, might think they could show me some compassion instead of dissuasion, and would offer their precious help so that I could reach adult age under the best conditions. A teenager is not a grown-up. A teenager can still be molded into some new type of person. It wasn't fear of their ghastly bait that prevented me from acting. It was disgust, and my need to keep intact my predisposition for the harmony of colors, for the right proportions, my sensitivity to touching, my keenness to odors. And, strange as it might seem, this required my doing nothing. Since it was from Stela that I inherited the intuition for the right form—which, under the circumstances, was telling me to act with caution, to stand back—that must have been the strategy that helped her hold on. Along with the inborn protocol of endurance we shared.

Still other fears were foisted on me, fears that were part of everyone's daily share. Who spoke a word to me one day about some thing that it would be better not to know? It wasn't quite clear what the exact nature of that thing might be. Some detail. Some development likely to further agitate my doubts concerning Mother's disappearance, replace them with other questions that I had not asked myself. That I would never ask myself. Any means of coercion served the good cause of those who embraced it.

That being so, I came to ask myself what exactly Mother's role was at the psychiatric hospital where she had been appointed after refusing to join more useful regiments. Even if she was a simple nurse and assistant to the doctor, would they not have tried to use her for other aims, aims, how to say, that better not be revealed to me? I've heard some say that Mother was spotless. Others, in hushed tones, spoke turns of phrase that didn't make any sense to me.

Rumor is an accomplice to fear. And rumors circulated endlessly about one person or another who contributed this way or that to reinforce our well-meaning order, as a warrant of safety and prosperity. I wanted, of course, in no way to question Mother's integrity. But could she have been forced into being used for some action or another because of how she cared for the pain of each and every? Because she wanted to protect me? Would she have been able to stick to her simple rules had I been menaced or used as some sort of hostage to impose pressure upon her?

Stela couldn't fail to notice that even healing could be turned into a weapon. How had she then determined what to do? How did she skip through the double bind? And what might she have done to earn her death or abduction? How might she have ended up being denounced?

Anyway, rumors and ruminations were of no use.

If her disappearance was indeed connected to the vague circumstances of her work at the hospital, her return did not elucidate that past any more than it did the present. In B. K.'s circle there was talk about collective compromise. His team's ostensible care for us, if I may say so, seemed to me a way of discharging themselves for their own involvement in spreading rumors of all kinds or whatever they might have done in the past beyond my or anyone's imagination. With no shame or guilt. But who'd care about such things now? There had been changes in the world since Mother vanished, changes of so many kinds. The virus that had altered our lives had mutated and was now spreading with more efficiency in new geographic configurations, developing new faces, new defenses. In the whirlpool of new terrifying events, few paid attention to such grotesque equivocations, and even less to their consequences. A page in history had been turned. Silence took up new inflections.

However, further rumors circulated after Stela's disappearance. They turned round and round inside my little head. If, after all, there had been an accident, two possibilities followed. Either the accident turned out to be a disguised suicide or she was, or could have been, skillfully led, or some might say helped, or perhaps simply pushed, to misstep and run into a car. But why such a trivial conspiracy against her? Stela had gone about her daily tasks without harming anyone, despite her diverging from the required sameness of idiom, gait, or thought. For some, however, these would have been good enough reasons.

That so many like her vanished, prey to phantom suspicions, attracted few people's attention outside of our area, partly because few cared and many still believed in ideals they never experienced, partly because disappearances had been staged, disguised in so many ways, strategies amended. Over time, reasons for suspecting individuals or placing them under more or less visible surveillance varied; categories establishing who was dangerous and why changed, as did the grounds on which exceptions from the rules were to be allowed. Some instructions about who was to be eliminated, transformed, or a combination of both, remained tucked away at the backs of drawers, while others had dissolved into dust or ashes. Most of them have never been put in writing. Later on, when such abrupt events as disappearances or accidents became more rare, more selective (and, as some have maintained, if not excusable, at least with less serious consequences), when the exceptions had been exhausted, the criteria became rather random, the procedures for keeping fear alive both more systematic *and* more chaotic. Everyone was likely to be caught in such an arbitrary drift net, Stela no less than many others.

(Suicide did cross her mind, yes it did, at times when she was overcome with exhaustion or when hope turned its back on her. But she carried so many along with her: their lives, their deaths. What would her life be without their lives, without their deaths? And what became of them if she stepped out?)

As a child, I would sometimes go with her to the psychiatric hospital where she worked. Through long corridors drenched with chloride and moans, through alleys overwhelmed with weeds, through mildewed basements inhabited by rats doomed to experiments whose purpose escaped me, she wore her smile. But when she fixed wires on the patients' foreheads and scalps, minding that they didn't get entangled in their hair, her smile faded away. And when the machine buzzed and she watched the vibrating wave patterns roll down in folds of graph paper, she seemed to be praying for the spikes and waves on the rolls of red-line paper not to disclose the patients' thoughts or dreams.

"We call this an electro-encephalo-gram. It helps the doctor see if patients are worried, or suffering some unseen pain."

" . . . telegram, you mean?"

"No, electro- . . . yes, telegram, say, a telegram of dreams."

The woman at the hospital's registration office always gave me a candy. On our way out, she never missed asking Mother about this or that patient, if "they were aaallrrright, dear? Have they taken their medication as prescribed? Have they, in due proportion?"

Within the aseptic perimeter of the hospital, what could I notice? But Stela? Wouldn't she eventually have chanced upon a misplaced needle (or vial), one day or another, noted a particular word spoken by a patient (or not)?

She was good, generous, genuine, too willing to help everyone. Many people were fond of her. Others didn't see that with a good eye. Not at all. Some still remembered the prodigy she had been before times had changed, the resonance of her violin—made by her mother's brother—in the National Radio Orchestra, her confident voice on the waves introducing programs for children. Others found her noxious. They didn't mind the violin smashed by the heroes of the new times, didn't mind the downgraded girl.

They remembered her father who owned an average-sized house and an old car of a foreign brand and was carried away because he spoke too much and not the right words at that. He didn't conform. He dressed like people in old movies, even when he was left with nearly nothing. He got what he deserved, in the end, covetous neighbors said.

Things could be as simple as that.

When you find yourself wandering in the midst of confusion and solitude, and one track leads to another, it's hard to know which is the good one. Or maybe you'd rather not know.

"Some of them are really in a bad way," Stela said one afternoon when she came home from the hospital more exhausted and upset than usual. "Beyond remission. That is," she explained, "it's when you can't go back where you were, to what you once were. That is, well, we'll talk about that later, when you grow up."

Later. Now. Before. At some point something must have happened to her. Was there anything wrong with Stela, now? Something that had brought her to a state beyond repair? Was that the reason she stayed so aloof? Something that might have affected not her body but, how to say, her spirit? Something simple with unabated effects and, clinically speaking, without remission?

Is it possible to act on someone's spirit without leaving traces on the body?

Stela's sedate gestures, her distant gaze, her reluctance to give me more details about her kidnapping, or abduction, seemed to speak from somewhere else: a place of accumulated detail she must have struggled to domesticate as long as she had been able to hold on.

Suddenly I understood and dropped all my former suppositions. Because it was enough to take the time to look at Mother.

And when I did, I saw the fatigue through which she moved, striving as well as she could to reach me, groping her way across the space between us, holding her arms out, adapting her pace to a staggering rhythm.

I held out my hands to her. She put something in my palms: pinkish-white, fleshy, humid matter. Soft, with creases and folds, held together by thin ruby threads.

Two uneven hemispheres slipped through my fingers, leaving a lukewarm print on my open palms. There was nothing I could do to stop them from dropping to the ground.

And wherever I am—standing, walking, running, indoors or out, in empty parks, on crowded streets, on the sea or on land, day or night—I hear the thump of that soft matter landing on the asphalt.

It lasts only an instant.

And in spite of its limp consistency, its temperature and damp surface, the form strikes the asphalt with a crack, the sound of an eggshell hitting the ground.

(The accident report did mention a crack in the right cheek-bone).

Still, Mother was so beautiful. Unconditionally so.

"And what of Stella have you missed most," B. K. asked me one day.

"Nothing to declare."

Nothing, simply that, far outside the perimeter of suspicion and fear, with my new name and my new habits, no one spots me as Stela's daughter.

Nobody here remembers Stela.

No one but me would have known Stela.

In the outlands, there is no one to share my dead with.

{10}

Notation

What prevented Mother from telling me the story of her abduction or detention? Something to do with our protectors? All I could do to learn more was to frustrate B. K.'s plan and tell him Mother needed to recover her strength. I would have to exercise a firm tone and, above all, avoid negotiations. And when, slightly raising his chin he acquiesced, we went for a walk, back to the Botanic Garden, to that bench where we had rested a while ago. From the large, slanting pocket of her trench coat Stela took out a notebook rolled up, no thicker than a tube or a small flute. When she unrolled it, its leaves were tattered, downy like peach skin. With her right hand, she smoothed out the first one, standing in for the lost cover—torn off by accident or on purpose—and then flipped through the pages. Lines of small letters unspooled quickly, as if in one long, long sentence. Here and there, I could make out other kinds of lines, traces of roads, cloud trails, watercourses, chimney smoke, and some small shapes, not unlike my own little sketchy figures, which seemed to take on a life of their own as the pages sped by.

How could I make sense of what was in there? The handwriting was small, twisted, shy. Suspicious of the page or, perhaps, even of her eyes, the letters must have hesitated to line up into words. Here, a spare alphabet slanted to the right, and farther on, other letters ran at briskly changing angles, as if they were written by another hand, or dictated by another mood. With a bit of luck, her improvised code had escaped the attention of her guardians and she somehow managed to find a new pencil once in a while. She could always maintain, if confronted by her abductors or caretakers, if someone had attempted to confiscate her notebook, that it was not letters to the outside or notes on what was happening she jotted down. Just doodles. That's it, doodles to while away the time. Her time there. She knew how to defend her lines. A habit, she'd say, that she had continued since childhood: watching time pass by, in her room at the end of the long corridor, away from the rubble of noise and fear during the war, and after, when another war broke out on the ashes of the former and the theater of operations turned inside. Let the crayon go, listen to a dog or a cat scratch the bottom of the door when the night smells of burnt cloth. It calmed her, it reassured her, nothing irremediable could happen on the page. No. She had no intention of sending whatever message to whoever might have been willing to receive one.

How could she? She was no longer, was she? Who then would care about her letters?

"I wrote to hide, not to reveal," she said in a hushed tone.

"But those lines kept me warm. The notebook was my home. I knew, yes, I somehow knew that I would find the strength to defend my right to it. Somehow. There must have been a way to."

She'd been left with nothing else.

Slow, graceful, her handwriting turned suddenly impatient, filled up the space of the page as if she wanted to make the most of what she had: on the face, on the back, and then, with another pencil, between her own lines.

"You know," she carried on, brushing off an iridescent insect that lingered on the page, "there was no hurry to write. No hurry to fill up the space left in the notebook. I wouldn't get another one for sure, or if I did, that would have implied an exchange for something I wouldn't bargain. So that making the most of what I had required caution and some inventiveness. From that point on, a new strategy imposed itself: to observe and describe in my mind, to keep the space left in the notebook as a last resort. Perhaps, someday I would somehow slip a letter to the outside into someone's hands or throw it over a fence.

"To tell the truth, I took a certain pleasure in thinking that they feared it, my writing in that overused notebook. Yes, that thought brought me some comfort. No matter how powerfully steeped in their position they appeared to be, a word, a sentence, as fractured or awkward as it might have been, could unnerve them. Their tiny power was not enough to rule out their fear, fear of another kind, but still fear. Diffuse, it infiltrated their nerves and tissues. Because they, too, had blood running through their veins, they had a child or a mother somewhere who had put their trust in them. But everything beyond their small world unnerved them, jeopardized their edifice: a letter to the outside, a phone call, a notebook in a drawer, a gaze. E-di-fi-ca-tion. A word that made me palm my ears. Ugly words can kill. And many of the ones they used, or shouted into loudspeakers in the street, or on the radio, sounded like an alien language to me. You brought one of those words home from school once and I slapped you in the face. I'm sorry, I couldn't help it. Of course, my rushed response surprised you and you took offense. It was beyond your understanding at the time. So many things were hard for you to understand. And some you'd better not. But you seem to have managed to sort things out by yourself. God knows how. It's still a mystery to me. It is. How some just do, others don't, or for whatever reason pretend not to."

A time came, Stela admitted, when she just ran out of words; and she ran out of patience keeping track of time by a simple system of vertical and horizontal bars she had devised, day after day scratched on the wall. For a while. Then the notebook became all about space. Fields and roads and rivers and mountains. There had to be someone along those roads, someone ready to overcome, avoid, or ignore obstacles in order to set her free. Someone with a smart dog would reach her in due course. And when that possibility, too, had been ruled out, she just sketched skinny figures to keep her company. Mother knew about the human body. Had looked at it inside and out. Had drawn its maps of sinews and veins. She had shown me how the body worked when she had no time to play with me. But, there, in her solitary notebook, the figures Stela had drafted while she was preparing for medical school had lost weight, they were only skin and bones, drained of life, drained of pain. Only lines, spirals, or circles remained of them. She sat there and figured out what kind of steps these imaginary friends would need to cope with the space that separated her from them. And so, the notebook became the home of a thin and busy population. Each had their role, their capability. Each had their rhythm of breath and speed, their feelings and moods, some, even a sense of humor. The figures in her notebook went about their daily routines in a choreography of sorts, but that, to her, was enough.

"The first ten years are tough," she heard once.

"Then, one learns how to live with it, more or less," said the voice in her light sleep.

{11}

An Accident

Rain fell in shreds and, as we walked the narrow dark streets paved with shiny, uneven cobblestones, on the other side of the river that crossed the city I could make out a row of pale gray structures, defaced, afflicted. Suddenly, we noticed one among them that reminded us of the huge building wrapped up in wisteria that B. K. had us visit. A flash of laughter rippled across Stela's composed features. Her startling laughter made me laugh, as well. It was good to share a laugh with Mutti. And when I turned my head back toward the street, the sun had begun to chase the clouds away.

We erred by the riverside.

Her laughter receded.

I laid my head in her arms and cried.

All the way through my crying, she spoke without pause, her breath a glass globe spinning round and round, slowly settling where my tears had been.

"When I was carried off it came as a relief.

"A devastating fatigue I'd been hiding all along. And now, the crowd, the heat were just too much.

"Yes, my life could take another turn if I vanished. Other than that, there's nothing spectacular to declare. It happened in a flash and, most certainly, without a witness to the scene. And had someone in the crowd caught a glimpse of a woman carried off in an ordinary car, what could they make of it? And whoever, by chance, might have happened *to want* to make something of it, what could they have done? Nothing could be undone. Nothing said.

"It happened to so many. I have no story to tell. There really wasn't one.

"There was instead a collision of matter: flesh, metal, plastic.

"Breath held for a while.

"Then, a dislocation of contours.

"It happened in broad daylight. In the middle of the boulevard. I made my way behind a dull, lethargic crowd that was forced to be there, forced to wait for someone or some event they weren't concerned with although it affected their lives deeply. At the decisive moment, they had to clasp their hands. In the eye of a distant camera, the scene was the performance of a grotesque script rehearsed over and over, or some improvisation played by extras, who mostly looked (many of them, felt) like extras of themselves. Or was it rather a form of calm resistance?

"The roofs are burning with dazzling light. My left hand in the pocket of my batiste dress with blue and green patterns, I'm holding a letter in my right hand, fanning my face with it, too visibly, now that I think about it. There's a harsh sound, brief, yet loud enough to catch my attention, to make me turn my head. At that exact instant, a gray car makes a loop, eludes other cars, bystanders, the crowd, then stops. A claw roots me out of the street, pulls my body toward the car. The door opens, making a soft sound. It shuts.

"Inside, another hand grabs me by my hair, pushes me onto the floor. Brown, dusty, reckless shoes—four of them—are pointing at me. The air inside the car smells of gasoline, acrid tobacco, perspiration. I barely feel the stream of blood running down my face. Where the stream splits into two lukewarm streaks, my face is cold ashes. My eyes burn. My face is a sheet of paper pierced by a cigarette, twice.

"Three minutes pass, four barely. Not long enough for anyone to notice a nameless woman being caught in a crowd's spiderweb, then dragged away in an ordinary gray car. And let's say my gaze did cross another's. Could I have laid a burden on those daring eyes? Dragged their stare along behind me in my misfortune? And what might have stirred in that dissident gaze? Fear, compassion, shame? Or simply stupefaction?

"My head pinned to the ground, I worry about how to pass on the letter now that I am stranded in that car. Not that I know the addressee any more than the sender. It came from far away—that much I knew—and it had to reach someone who was even farther.

"Someone's hopes were in that letter. A woman's, perhaps, stranded somewhere in the wilderness. Or behind bars.

"But when the car arrives at its destination, nothing matters anymore.

"Suddenly it's winter. In my light dress, thinned by the sun, soiled by dust and blood, I'm cold. The cold sticks to my skin. I cannot feel my skin. Someone took it as I came through the car door, I think, with a rapid turn of a hand. I have nothing else than the cold for cover. Beneath the cold, something burns. Deeply. And I wonder what will remain of me when the fire has died out. I laugh in sharp spurts. Now and then. Inside and outside. For this and that. For almost nothing.

"There's a river, high, yellow-green, murky near where I've been brought to spend my life. Thin snakes ripple its surface, over and over, a gauze of flies obscures my view. Wheat grows on the earth-made walls of my shelter. It grows up high. Thick dust saturates the air round about. It alleviates the cold.

"Then, there are days when you still feel alive. And on days like that, more than violence, it was a cunning normality I feared, which crept into my life by degrees. With it came the concern they showed for me, surfacing little by little in their tone, in their oily smiles, their slimy faces.

"No, not all of them were brutal. Not always. They were not always violent. A sap-like kindness budded in their voice, welled up in their gaze, now and then. Their aim was, after all, not to eliminate me. Change my nature was what they hoped to do. Their good intentions were unbounded. I thought of you, my child, I did. Not all the time. Not too much. I could feel your name drop on my lips, letter by letter, or through the window of my small room I might see your face against the glass, thinned by the rain, my hand trying to reach you from the other side, my fingers touching only that flat and icy shape. And then, one day, I couldn't make out that face any longer, couldn't make the sound. Your name, I couldn't remember your name, Cora.

"In der Ferne warst du meine Schatten Tochter (und es war Kälte, und es war Müdigkeit) . . . . ist es doch—mutterlich? . . . Mutterlicht. . . .

"In some remote place, a heavy, muted sound dropped to the ground. And I feared you were no longer looking for me. You had your continents and oceans to explore, after all. Had I gone missing so that you could find your way alone, I wondered?

"During my allotted walking time one day, I came across a small object made of cast iron, bent, disfigured. I brushed the dust off it with the hem of my skirt and hid it in my pocket. It looked like a small handgun, but they'd know it wasn't what it looked like. Escaping confiscation, the smashed doorknob joined my few belongings, sibling to the one I'd once spotted, not far from our home, in the unsettled ground of what was no longer a street but a pile of detritus. A doorknob, smashed flat, from the absent door of a demolished house. It had shined in the dust, that doorknob from my other life, on the morning I was making my way through the old district to hand over the letter. That cherished oldest district in the city, from which all past was about to be effaced. Skip trucks excepted, the place was deserted. Houses crumbled to dust, draining the streets of shadows. The inhabitants had been ousted, passersby chased off by the stifling, sanitary odor of renewal. Out of nowhere, a toddler popped up, showing interest in splinters and wires. What happened to the district of dust, I often wondered in my new constricted life. Had weeds invaded it before it turned into a monstrous area? Were the abandoned scaffolds still haunting the city's riverbanks? Had its hallucinating stray dogs found a shelter? And the former inhabitants, the young, but mostly the old, were they still crumbling along the corridors of their new dwellings, narrow, dark, unending? Did the splinters keep flashing in the toddler's dreams?

"But then I'd wipe them all out of my mind and return to my new sketchy companions.

"What happened to the district mattered little after a while.

"Nothing meant more than finding out how to go on with my new life, from one day to another."

Yellow Fields Are Still Fields

At some point in her story, I stopped crying. She put the back of her hand on my burning forehead, then brushed it with her lips.

On deserted roads, she gropes for her way along a thin rope, her ankles wrapped up in the cotton of the night
Lonely, as only the night can be

"Through the fog that toned down the dark, I suspected there were mountains beyond the path I took," she continued. "And closer to my eyes, I could see strange architectures, roads, a riverbank. The high-powered beam of a searchlight, rooted somewhere I couldn't see, revolved intermittently, giving my surroundings a more distinct face for an instant before the passing cone of light expanded every shape, leaving behind a darkness that effaced all contours.

"Standing still, I felt suddenly elsewhere, and later, in my small room, I would let the two landscapes unfold in my mind: the congenial darkness, then the glowing beam. Two hemispheres, each the half of the other, both part of a whole, or of what we imagine to be a whole. One view overlapped with the other, mountains, strange architectures, thick darkness, all on a turning stage."

She moved her arm slowly from under my head, dipped her fingers into the river, touched my burning forehead. It cooled down and I felt safe. Under the obstinate sun, the river seemed to have sunk deep down between its banks. Her voice rose from somewhere as deep as the bottom of the river, while her hands undulated above its surface. If her face had remained so surprisingly unchanged, her voice, its syncopated intonation, was suddenly unsettling. It struck me like a stray wave in my mind. Yes, from the moment she started speaking, her voice sounded more like that of a stranger, because that was it: I could not remember, I no longer remembered Mother's voice.

"The field where I was allowed to walk during the day, weather permitting, was scorched, wide open, hopeless," Mother explained.

"I followed at random a band of clear light, an intermittent sound of water that seemed to run underground, mingling with the rustle of the few trees which bordered the field. Soon it turned out that such signs could be trusted. Days on end I walked, sniffing the air, feeling my way, vigilant at every move, before I came upon a large ailanthus tree standing alone in the open field, a few steps away from a small stream that revived the scorched landscape. Sitting there, between sparse tufts of grass, my toes dipped in the refreshing water, I observed the other side of the stream, so different from the bands of life I could see on my routine walks on this side, something that looked more like an inner core, solid and dense, around which layers in motion were driven by a force that I had once been part of. A sloping road led to an untidy garden. A house in the distance with windows and walls, like all houses, and a huge, dark wooden door that like a mocking mug gaped at me. A dog's cage, awkward and huge. Bales of hay, round, indolent. And above them, terraced hills covered in vines and fields turning yellow in the sun.

"Now and then everyday sounds reached me, mixed with hooves that resonated from the ground, proofs of life going on somewhere on the other side of the stream. That life that I heard crackling on the other side reached me like the waves of an old radio sowing discord in my thoughts, which I had, by then, tamed as much as I could. Or so it seemed.

"From that day on, I walked with a purpose: to reach that spot and to sit by the water, until slowly, toward the end of the summer, most of it had been evaporated by the heat. To sit there and embrace with my eyes all that was on the other side: vineyards, yellow fields, road, garden, house, dog's cage. Then, eventually, I would turn my eyes back to the thin stream, which only a while ago had seemed an enormous gap, the only obstacle, other than my fear, keeping me from the facing bank, almost a ditch by now.

"For some time I had been visited by the idea that, if the reasons for my kidnapping (or whatever one calls it) remained beyond my grasp, for my captors these reasons must have been equally obscure. My guardians, or keepers, themselves must have ignored the reasons for their hate, or fear, or whatever command-ed their acts. Were they even aware that they acted in the name of a saving evil? But, really, what they believed in was not a matter of concern for me, it was, rather, the effects of their belief: the houses that had crumbled to dust, the displaced inhabitants van-ishing along the dark corridors of their collective living quarters, their bodies numb, their breath slowed down by fatigue, their si-lence unending. As for my guardians (or protectors, as they called themselves), what else could they do but stick to their empty phrases, to the small power they had been granted?

"Such simple thoughts, which hadn't budded in my mind before, were heartening. Finding the weak spot of my guardians mattered to me as much as finding mine mattered to them. But, for my part, I wasn't interested in turning their weak spot against them, just in using it as a prop I could hold onto as long as I had to in order to stay sane.

"One day marked by no particular sign other than a gray sky and an icy grip in the back of my neck, the barking of the dog reached my ears in broken notes, as if it was trying to send its high-pitched voice over a tall obstacle, too high for its size, or perhaps too far away. With the barking of that dog, which I couldn't see, tame, or pet, a new possibility began to form in my confused mind: not that I had been abducted, but that I had, *au fond*, been sent to this place, wherever it was, as if—as if I had a mission of sorts.

"That possibility developed into certitude in spite of a detail that had puzzled me from my first days there: in fact, and against all reason, there was nothing I had been asked to do or even say. I wasn't forced to give any information (there wasn't much I was equipped with, anyway, at least nothing of interest to my keepers and whoever had hired them). Neither was I made to do forced labor, as others have been, to expiate concocted faults.

"Nothing. That's what I was to do there. Nothing.

"In other words, my mission—if any—consisted not in naming, but in keeping silent. Compared to that of others, mine was a lucky lot, after all.

"Yes, I started to understand that was why I had been brought there: to spend time, to spend my time on earth, silently, to exhaust my pernicious thoughts. Lying there in the grass by the stream that day, hands cupped under my head, I weighed the consequences of this new possibility. Hope slowly chased the clouds away from my tired spirit.

"Just like the revolving beam of the searchlight which had changed my perspective of the dark's architectures, that insight marked a decisive turn in my life. From then on, everything happened in a rush tempered only by my extreme attention to every move, to every gesture, second by second. I wouldn't go as far as calling what followed a choice, and even less was it an act of rebellion. Anyone honest enough or relatively well informed knows that such claims are nothing but vainglory. And vainglory was my captors' coat of arms. Take it away, what's left of them? As far as I was concerned, I had to keep on breathing. I had to let my breath settle down, to seize the exact moment when the searchlight flipped the view of the surroundings like a sudden eclipse, the exact moment when light turned into haze, fear into composure.

"Then, shadow and light rotated, the dangerous beam transformed the leaves of the ailanthus tree into bright goldenrod half-moons. Soon they were no more than a rustle in the dark.

"I stood up and knew I could do it.

"I knew that in the brief interval between glowing light and sheer darkness, one leap was enough to get me over the stream, over the threshold of the perimeter.

"One unwavering step, one leap was enough for me to pass to the other side, given a certain disposition of air, a certain geometry of humors, a passing blindness of the searchlight. It was enough to hold my breath, to pass over with no theatrical gesticulation, to ignore the brittle sound of hooves.

"For an instant—one instant reverberating in my mind ever

since—my arms at a slight distance from my hips, chin up, feet above the ground, I escaped my own weight.

"What was on the other side no longer mattered.

"Twenty weeks doesn't seem that long.

"Twenty weeks can turn into a life sentence.

"Because, as it soon turned out, what was on the other side did matter. Returning has proved no less risky than escaping. And nobody had to know about where I had been, how I escaped, or why they'd closed their eyes to let me go. Nobody, not even you. Above all, not you, my child. At the hospital, someone would help me fit in again, and life would just go on. It had to. There was you, there was Grandmother, and the household to run. Yes, they must have closed their eyes. The perimeter of fear had to have some leeway for the system to function and to preserve its credibility for the outside. Released or repentant, I was an even better instrument in their hands, or so they hoped."

{13}

Hesitation

The bright sun had washed out the walls of the old city houses still standing and gave them a glare which almost hurt the eyes. When we passed the gate of the graveyard, the stones and the tree trunks were sharing that glare. Something solid in that day's light dissolved all fears. Even a single tear wavering in the corner of the eye would change its mind before it dropped. As we took a narrow path dappled with light, Mother put her right hand on my shoulder and turned her eyes toward the profile, carved in stone, of a young girl facing our family lot, where Grandmother was buried some years after Stela disappeared.

Mother glanced at me, then back at that stone portrait:

"Orphan girl. More lonely and abandoned than we have been, with only weeds to keep her company. It's poor comfort, dear Cora, I know, but let me tell you: what you've just heard has happened to countless others. It has. It might have happened to this girl's family, since no one has cared for her grave in years, nor lit a candle for her soul."

She looked at the gravel on the path between the two lots as if counting each pebble, or giving it the attention it deserved.

"People vanished in a snap, a hocus-pocus. More stories than the beads in Grandmother's amber necklace slumber at the bottom of the river that runs through the city and, farther, into a canal, then into a dark sea."

"Why did they step out, Mother? Or why were they forced to?"

"Who knows? On account of honor, faith, or, perhaps, to keep safe someone they loved. Some couldn't cope with the cold, or lacked in fortitude. Others were mowed down by their fellows' envy, ignorance, or lack of honor. Still others, because of misunderstandings. Sooner or later, they've all been muffled by layers of silence. A few had the chance to run away. But who would listen to them wherever they went? Outside the perimeter of fear, silence ruled in different ways, but it was still silence, and more often than not indifference."

She lit a thin unbleached beeswax candle by the profile of the young girl carved on the moss-green stone. Then she turned to our family lot. "Grandmother doesn't have a picture here, on the cross, does she? You should think of having one printed on a marble oval and fix it in there. Someone will do it for a few pennies. We don't want her to be abandoned, like that girl over there."

The wax dripped on her fingers.

A strange celebration, there, for the two of us.

I had never seen a tear in Mother's eyes before.

And it wasn't to last. She raised her hand to reach my forehead, drew a wisp of hair behind my ear, where she thought it belonged.

"But you, you shouldn't worry, my child. You have something to do, and you will do it as well as you can."

The profile carved in stone remained still, grew smaller and smaller behind a curtain of small flying creatures. I had promised Stela we'd go back to the Botanic Garden.

The Scar of a Moment

We got there late since it had taken me some time to ask again for permission to take some time off from the program established by B. K. Guardians in faded brown uniforms ran up and down the Garden's alleys whistling closing time. Before the last call, Mother raised her eyes toward me and tucked her hands into the pockets of the lime green trench coat she insisted on wearing despite the warm weather.

I standing, she sitting, Stela seemed so much smaller than I.

At once, her face began to dilate, growing longer, then larger, until it reached the enormous size of a full moon projected on the darkening sky, an unmapped territory where I could see open pores, thin vessels, lines, trajectories. Then they all dissolved into a smooth surface, a huge flat disk on the night's screen. The larger her face grew, the more volume drained from it, and from that colossal flat translucent disk came a soft comforting voice, spelling out words without haste, without distress:

it was   *like here*   *but otherwise*

She leaned back on the bench, took her hands out of her pockets, then got up. The guardians' whistles urged us to the exit. This was no time for explanations. We left the Botanic Garden five minutes before closing. B. K. expected us for one more apartment visit. But the anger that had spurred me on in there burst out in the commotion of the street. I turned my head away from her, in the direction of the guardians behind the railings, looking out over the ignorance of the passersby and the cars in the street. I can't say why, instead of putting my anger aside and my arms around her shoulders, why now a voice locked in my chest for so long forced its way out.

It was a matter of life or death. I was not raging against her, but against everything. Against what was happening now, and back then, and after. And I had no one closer to share that anger with. It was my way—the only way I'd found—to tell Mother how I missed her.

A wild howl broke from my throat. Yes, as she said, it wouldn't last but an instant.

Then, with the lightness of breath,
dust rose above our eyes
and when of the sun remained only the scar of a moment
remembered behind the lid
an impression of white hung there
              impatient
not an omen   more like an open lung
something slippery that does not sustain the word

She stepped back, like a child caught in the wrong, looked over her shoulder for an instant, and then her dilated, gold green eyes stared at me, as the slow waves of her voice were reaching my ears from some remote place:

i was there   and i was ashes

I looked Mother in the face. Her lips were tight. The voice carried on. The more I looked at her the smaller she got.

Soon she is no more than a dancing spot fading away

STANDING,
WALKING,
RUNNING

{1}

Water & Snow

Head above the thermal source, I swim and watch the snow fall. Some hundred sixty pounds of bones and flesh held by seventy percent water.

Out of the baths, I walk into the winter. Shades of white turn into horizontals, rising lines, shivering figures. Indigo shadows spread out as I walk and leave trails of myself behind. I step on that fleeting pattern, silver-white puffy matter filling in my footprints sooner than expected. Fresh prints grow in no time, the fugitive's misfortune. But who'd care about footprints now?

So many snows I've been in. Their afterimage, an old film. Doctored, scratched. And where once a face was, a constellation of dark spots covers the film now, bulges, cracks. Eyes roll upon a wing, a bright disk overcomes the figure in the foreground, ungainly animals head to unknown destinations. Snow is a phone call. A girl left behind. A dog howling. It's but another face of water, for a while.

In time, I have become lighter.

"But I agree with you, I do," Cora says, then stops, gasps for air, and carries on her warm-up, one leg stretched on the balcony rail, top of head on toes: a geometric puzzle.

"When it comes to it," she manages to get the words out as she twists her limbs. "Yes," she nods, "the body is a drag."

Cora breaks her motion, folds one arm on the wooden bar, leans her head on it, soft as a cat's sleep. She is very pale at the shoulders, as far as I can see, but I don't mind that, and, wrapped around her hips, a T-shirt notifies anyone not sensible enough to have already noticed it that behind every gifted cat there's often a rather talented woman. Cora moves as if she had something to exhaust in herself, fear, doubt, loss.

Perhaps I walk in the wrong direction, but home is not where I want to head yet. I have more of this translucent blue on white surface to investigate before it gets dark. You see, I am a man of minimal requirements and I carry with me all I need: eyes alert to surfaces, skin sensitive to wind, legs solid enough to handle distance.

In the studio, our temporary residence, she works out and waits. She waits for the summer and a letter in the mail. The space of the studio is small. I'm more of a hindrance when she does her routines, though she'd rather have me there, in a corner, the only witness of her commitment to aerial exploration.

"It is an arithmetic fact, when you think of it," (twists left calf, drops right arm with a fold) "all in all there's no one, no one, Luca, to try my weight against, to work out new steps with. Nobody adds up, no company, but you. Luca, just watch, tell me what you see when I do that twist."

And as she spins, bubbling words spiral from her dry lips and I evaluate the possibilities I have to double myself in case she needs a larger audience, though, in truth, the gaze she's looking for is far too far away to reach. But, when I think of it, she can be quite good company to herself. Brave girl, who's coped with so much space, like a smart dog. Did what she had to and couldn't do without. Then found me, inadvertently.

"Luca, are you listening at all?"

I was, more than she would want to know, my head on her throbbing chest at night. A hollow combination of slippery muscles suspended in seventy percent liquid. Water is where she feels good, she says, when she doesn't have to hold on to her feet (toes, heels, arched soles) or when she can no longer hold on to the air (though, in more than one way, she is ever so good at it). Her long arms stretched along my chest feel like a huge bird's wings, resting after a long journey. Then, some nights, a small bird settles on my chest, white, serene.

What happens when we sleep, I wonder? How are the snippets of yesterday's film edited? What shapes does the weightless body unfold? And what remains of them on our gloomy floors, what ghosts of our daily gestures (or is it the other way round, our gestures the ghosts of the night's events)?

And then, when I am about to crack the code of her heartbeats, she dreams out loud:

"If water is what we are about, how much of Stela runs through my veins?"

I hold Cora in my arms to comfort her and dissipate my own fear. Because I fear, I do, that her blood will start dripping from the tips of her fingers, then pool at my feet, as she once told me her mother's did at her own feet, in a dream. A melancholy fact. But melancholia isn't good. It has me stuck in a corner, and, like her, I have to walk, run, keep going.

She tucks her head into my armpit, folds her legs into the warm cotton sheets. And even in her sleep, she asks, "Luca, what shall I do?" although she knows the answer so much better than I do. Mostly, I think she's certain about what she'll never do. Cora, too, is a woman (though I still call her the girl) of minimal requirements: space to do her routines and to listen to layers of silence, someone to talk to (awake or in her sleep), a company of dancers with whom to fit her step patterns.

Every so often, she stands up at night and walks to the end of the bedroom, her palms feeling the dark, stretching along the wall, testing air, wood, glass. It comes without intent, she says, then in a flash, a long narrow strip of fabric unwinds around her spine, looks for a way out. But what am I trying to make sense of? There's nothing to decrypt in her pacing the dark. Just keep close to her. Foresee her next step. Stand by her, for she has no one else to trust.

I pull a leg out of the snow. Then the other.
Things are not as difficult as they appear.

{2}

Untitled

(Unknown destination),
ca. 1992, installation, 16mm film,
two television monitors, two glass stands

Other than the television monitors on stands facing the viewer at eye level, the room is empty. The same footage (black-and-white, eye-level shot) is running on both monitors in a loop, with only a vague variation in the image grain and the speed of the footage (one loop lags slightly behind the other). A nonchalant woman of an uncertain age, her shoulders and arms covered by a three-quarter-sleeve dark cardigan, makes slow progress on the surface of a moving walkway, or so it seems. In spite of the weight she carries in one hand (a suitcase? a box?), she radiates an ease that messengers do when they bring news which will untangle some old knot. The woman stands out in a mass of pallid figures. As she closes in (three quarters of her figure in view), a long shadow passes over her face, then exits the frame. Had she lifted her sunglasses over her forehead, her expression might have taken a different turn at that point. But, as the slow mechanism carries her along, the woman's hair, just covering her ears, barely wavers, while her face remains unnaturally smooth. Only her cardigan beats the air as if stirred up by a breeze or—as the scene was most likely shot in an airport corridor—by a rush of mechanically circulated air, something unnatural, fabricated. Her face draws closer, gets larger, and when it has almost covered the screen and her lips are about to sketch an imperfect circle, a freeze-frame marks a pause. Then the movement carries on, but inversely, from front to back, more briskly now, briskly accompanied by the hissing of a tape's static. The woman's gestures, fluid just a moment ago, suddenly seem to crumple, until only a visual echo remains of her silhouette.

Then: a blank screen and, before the cycle resumes, a few lines unfold, white letters on a black background:

> *water equals time*
> *&*
> *provides beauty*
> *with its double*

3

Suddenly, One Day

A jittery guardian butted in on my siesta, grumbling something about the showroom. What's gone wrong? The television monitors were set up to play the piece in a loop throughout the opening hours of the tourist season, weren't they? Still, he said, at the reception room there is a call for the man who put the piece together, or made it, or is in charge of it. Someone wanted to see me. Some urgent matter. Not technical. I had to go.

The odd steps she made resonated on the wooden floor. Soft, feline, watchful, the pace of someone trained to avoid danger. In her gaze, I seemed to be some distant spot on the horizon. But, as she was nearing, a sudden glimmer changed her expression.

In the adjoining room, the monitors had been put to sleep. It was closing time.

Her dress, light as her shadow, concealed, to some degree, a sketch of legs. A bell-shaped, purple silk dress, a trace of tie-dye, brushing her heels. In the door frame, the girl was a fleeting portrait: "Green scarf & amber hair." Her syllables were round, transparent, in spite of a dust cloud that would have drifted in her voice had it had the time. But she was not there to converse.

All she wanted to know was where I found Stela.

The woman on the screen.

Her mother.

4

Chance Encounters

On the road, seeking out Stela, for twenty-some years. There's no time limit for such a thing.

At noon, there had been poppies, radiant on the rim of the road. Now they were preparing for their night journey. Often, the sky speaks for such situations, but today its blue and orange tones have faded unnoticed. Only the bouquet of the fields persists: grass, mint, mustard. If she ever imagined this encounter, it must have flashed through her mind as a storm of emotions, raw, unfiltered, unlike mine ruled by restraint, caution, and a generosity I've had to forgo. But did I ever think that she, too, would run away, or that we would meet again? Even if I had, it hardly mattered. For the moment, the point was not that she had found me, but that she'd found Stela. By now, so many possibilities had been exhausted, with regard to our lives, or to the versions of Stela's story we had put up together. In the early evening, the silence was hard to break. Then something clear and deep in her voice burst out, a combination of sounds I had never heard before that evening when our paths crossed again in this forsaken village populated by fixed and moving figures, by artists from all over. It was a tone of voice that hardly matched her spare build.

Events had occurred, yes. Some had taken longer than others, and now, how could I believe that the girl who insisted on knowing where and how I filmed the woman on the screen was the same girl I once knew, my next-door neighbor, or the too candid daughter of my next-door neighbor, a woman of a rare presence? The girl she made me think of had a mole on the back of her hand, below her thumb. I had teased her about it long ago. But when I had forgotten all about the girl (more or less), that birthmark stayed with me, and how I once drew close to it with my camera, left nothing else in the frame but her hand's dilated pores and that flat hazelnut eye. Now I perused her hand: a pink, apricot surface crossed by pale violet streaks, and a faded brown spot at the root of her thumb. A vibration animated her wrists. Her hands were a white blur when she began to talk, at last. They said more than her words.

She looked like Stela, and she didn't.

She moved slower than the cloud above our heads. A solid cloud. The evening breeze was now filling up her silk dress.

It wasn't the change in her that surprised me. She still fit into her teenaged frame. It was space. There had been so much of it, in her life, in mine, between us. Flowing patterns. Weather of all kinds.

But changes aside, I remembered that long ago, perhaps even before I set eyes on her, the girl had withdrawn into a tunnel to cry out her anger, with no one to hear her. Then she happened upon these hands, these long legs, this fine neck, these supple wrists and ankles—and so many possibilities of space she could explore.

What did it matter now if there was no one to listen to her? What mattered was breathing. Breathing and digging that tunnel had brought her here at last. Circumstances did the rest. Luck, too, if she ever had any, and I imagine she must have.

Sometimes, at night, when she left my home for hers, I made sketches of young Cora hiding in a tunnel, then crawling through it, all the muscles of her thin body tightened to get her out. They were awkward moves and only hers, yet in so many ways they resonated with the ones I made in my own tunnel. Men in faded uniforms must have come across those sketches, and many others, when they inspected (and emptied) my house shortly after I had received, at last, my traveling papers, and left her and everything else behind. One of them might have wondered if there was some code or secret message hidden there before making up his mind that he had nothing to report: piles of paper, just garbage, and to the garbage they would go.

The tunnel: her only space to breathe. And mine, too, in the dry winter that followed Stela's disappearance.

My Vantage Point

In the provinces, many borders behind us now, where we both once lived, I was the conspicuous neighbor. Someone who should have stayed away from their unlucky household. But, eventually, I became an ally to the daughter. For a while. I was the neighbor before I became her confidant. The one who heard their dog howl himself out of breath, heard Stela's mother drop the shutters, heard the gate squeak all day long for a while, people opening and shutting or slamming it behind them, men in dark gray suits, and others, men and women who didn't seem to be part of the family.

Then it calmed down, the turmoil following the accident (everybody knew, had heard, concluded it had been an accident, had seen the flock dressed in black come and go, the priest dip his frock in the summer rain pools, the not-so-old grandmother do her best to run the household—with intermissions). And when night fell and restlessness drifted from the street into the corners of their house, I heard the wailing sounds (was I the only one?) coming not from the grandmother but from the dog. And when that too stopped, the girl came to my house, shared her worries with me for a while, rejected the story of the accident. She'd thought up her own story, compared it with my amendments, took care of my dog and garden when I went out to train my eye taking photographs of inoffensive landscapes, which didn't risk having my camera confiscated, as it had been before.

When the traveling permit arrived, at last, I walked out on her. I had to. There wouldn't be another chance to leave and do with my life what I had to. As for the girl, she had to grow up, figure things out by herself, get on without me. In time, she would come to think of her former neighbor as a chance encounter. Or forget me altogether. I hoped my dog would stand by her, a consolation for the one she'd lost. After all, not much had happened between us. Hadn't I been there just to help her out of the tunnel? There was nothing more I could afford to do for the girl. I was tied to my life as she was to hers and to that of her surviving grandmother, before she lost her too. My work alone was to keep me alive, away from intruders, and that involved running as far as I could. Over time, she, too, would realize she could risk giving herself another life, and, with a bit of perseverance and chance, she'd find out how to do it.

But I did carry something of her with me. How could I not? Not an object, not even a photo or one of those sketches, only flashes of the way she leaned her head on her shoulder, the circles she drew with her hands to prove she was there, the angle of light on the porch of their house one early morning, in September.

Eventually—at what point I cannot say—the house, the street, the city's anatomy faded, blanked out, or the place where I kept them just hurt less.

{6}

Reels

Two boxes of reels! I found them not far from the border, when, past the customhouse, past questions and searches, I was "approved for the road." My heart still racing, a knot throbbing in my throat, I parked my Škoda on the shoulder and walked around to stretch, to take in the new air, to feel the mild snow under my soles. I looked back at the curtain of fear that had dropped behind me still wondering that I had managed to pass, and saw nothing but the dismal customhouse behind the aseptic offices of the new country. From where I stood, on the other side of the border, having just stepped out of my life into another, mine all the same, I could still make out the two angular silhouettes fighting boredom in the gloomy space of their office. Two beardless boys appointed to guard the border, as thin as their machine guns and ill at ease in their worn-out uniforms the color of mud.

Everything over there, where I came from, remained small, coated with dust.

But why linger over that thought? I stamped to warm up my feet, to feel my new space. I crushed out a cigarette and hit something solid with the point of my shoe. A stone? Ice? No, the sound said: metal. I knelt down and realized I had stepped on two boxes brimming with film coiled on reels, shiny and black as the sky that showed through the balding forest at the edge of the road. Two boxes covered by mud mixed with snow, sending icy signals to my fingers. Someone must have had an interest in those boxes and then, maybe, disappointed, threw them away, or, from the other side, someone rolled them under the barbed wire or bowled them (when the guards were dozing or pretending to? did the guards do it, in exchange for some small present, say, a bribe, or a day off? and if it was not the guards who passed them over the border, what happened to the one who did? why hadn't anyone bothered to pick them up? did something go wrong? did someone pass them over the border precisely for them to find their way into a solicitous hand? and what kind of story had those films recorded? what for?).

In any event, there was no point in me caring about them when I had other worries. My rough coat was of no help against the gray cold I carried from beyond the border and into my every cell. A porcupine entangled in frozen leaves and moss was feeling its way out, exploring its surroundings. A car dashed by my left side, followed by a restlessness of branches: someone might have been watching me from over my shoulder, but no, it was just a rush of wind. "Time for me to go," I thought, even if, at least for a while, no clock dictated my schedule. I tucked the boxes into the tiny free space left in the back of my car loaded with more than one would need for the three week journey abroad which my travel permit allowed. I would, no doubt, pass other checkpoints along my way, but no one there would care for such trivia as the two boxes of film.

I pulled into the first gas station for a few small things: a drink of water, a decent lighter, change to make a phone call. Everything small. Basic. A whiff of soap and detergent emanated from the place. The gasoline smelled better, or so it seemed. But I had to be watchful. As I tried to make sense of dialing area codes and using the appropriate coins, a man appeared to be more than casually curious to observe what I was about to do. And what would he suspect? That I would go on with my life, I suppose, illicitly, because that's what a defector does, goes on, ears still filled with the dog's panting behind the car, the dog's small, sand-colored eyes watering, his body fighting through the dust raised by the rushing wheels, the dog all trust and muscle, eventually fading out of sight, a body of dust.

Then I entered the bar. "Ein Glas Wasser, bitte," were the first words I uttered. Never had language seemed so clear, unhindered. And, at once, I was given what I'd asked for.

{7}

At dawn, the silhouette of a Weimaraner—breath to bone—draws a dotted line parallel to the horizon.

{8}

Loops

"So, you are Stela's daughter."
"I once was."

She pointed at something in the distance. As she spoke, the light in the room changed to pale lavender. Her fingers were thin and white. You could hang a wet scarf on them, let it dry in the summer air.

A bright disk overcomes the figure in the foreground. Ungainly animals head to unknown destinations. Snow is a phone call. A girl left behind. A dog howling.

"After you left (a few days later, I think, for no one in the otherwise watchful neighborhood could say exactly when you'd snuck away), your dog stopped by our house for a while. He coiled up in Domenica's deserted corner before breaking away forever. I knocked at the gate of your house: locked and barred. I ran up and down the streets. 'Luna, Moni, Malu, Domenica,' I cried out, reciting along with his name a requiem to all my dogs and only friends before I met you, my allies in tracking Stela. At some point his name slipped from my mind, along with—you will forgive me—that of his owner."

"A dog can trespass but not defect, Cora. Even taking you along was not an option."

"It might have—I don't know—it might have, but, you see, it really doesn't matter anymore."

"Nothing else was an option, under the circumstances, Cora. Nothing. Leaving everything behind weighed heavily on me, how could it not? But I had to give myself the chance for another life, or try to. And that's a journey one can only make alone. You, too, have had that situation to consider, and as I understand, you only took to the road when there was no one left for you to leave behind. But, look, my dear, you've managed: you've danced yourself out of the place . . . like Baryshnikov!"

"Yes. Just about."

{9}

The Reels

had other things on my mind at that time of trial and error, after my one-way journey past the border: find a roof, some food, get the car going, get myself going, get the papers. Appointments and deadlines and other appointments. Papers of different colors allowing for different periods of residence in the new country, for a different range of activities. Two metal boxes of dark reels turn out to be of no help in such situations. They're not useful currency, so far as I know. Yet, if only as a reminder of the future promised by that unending night when I crossed the border, I've carried them along with me, storing them in basements, back-street sublets, walk-ups, interim studios, trusting there was some material on the reels I could use as *objets trouvés*. Wasn't it what they were? I did consider the possibility that they'd been left there for me to find. But who'd have put them in my way? And why? Or that someone might have just lost them on their way out of the homeland, their thoughts as frozen as mine, their chest as tight.

The lost keeps the found in equipoise, said a tobacco-colored newspaper clipping I had tucked in one of the boxes, because at one point, perhaps, it helped me make sense of my attachment to a hank of celluloid.

Years passed. I became less of a nomad. Resting on a shelf in what was now my permanent studio, the boxes were covered in dust of many varieties, the reels lagged behind current technology, parts of them defaced by mute chemical reactions. And when I finally unwound them, what was there to see? Not much. Yards of people going about ordinary tasks, type-lettered captions on celluloid spelling out:

—the time at which they left the house and when precisely they returned (hour, minutes on the dot);

—with whom they had exchanged a word, a gaze (or not);

—how many boxes of matches they had bought, how many packs of chalk or pairs of underwear (above or under the counter, local or foreign brand), how many pounds of sugar, oil, salt.

Yes, salt, more than anything else.

But what, I wondered, were they all carrying under the burden of those bags of rare victuals, under their stiff winter coats?

What kinds of innerness?

What lining of fear, diffidence, humiliation? What moments of sudden awareness?

As they came and went sinking into the unending piles of snow, shoulders bent, arms unhinged by the weight they carried, their lives turned around a spindle—invisible like the eavesdropping microphones and eagle-eyed cameras that tracked the black-and-white women, men, children, zooming in on every facet of their lives by day or by night. There must have been something small, though, in each person's pocket, around the neck, in the lining of the rough coat—a tiny rusted key, a photograph (faded, dog-eared), a piece of cloth, a silent watch—some reminder of who they once were, they or their parents, a friend or a cellmate. Leftovers of what they'd buried, burned, dropped into the gutters to stay above suspicion (a pack of letters, a diary, a wedding ring, a handful of golden coins). The rest of their lives they carried on their shoulders.

From where I was, in time and space, that spectrum of grays and browns (lead, ash, thirsty earth, bloodless bone, loaded sky) seemed out of place, futile, and fake at that. And yet, wouldn't I know it wasn't? Would my skin not still itch at the sight of them in their rough coats, shoveling piles of snow? Was I not still wearing the rash on the back of my neck? Did I not still feel the weight of my conscript coat, its plastic collar, hear the inner conflagration of early mornings when I slipped my hands into the dark tunnel of its stiff sleeves? Would not my heartbeat be quickened by the stifling muteness of those misty figures, by their thick slow motion and restrained gestures, their ghostly steps? Would my chest not still tighten at the possibility of some technical error hurling me back into that film just when I'd safe-ly got to the end of the paperwork releasing me from its frames? In spite of my unease, I was far away and safe. And yet, I could not keep the reels from running on and on, nor let those figures plod vainly in that landscape perverted by mud and wreckage. No, I could not let the dark, forlorn silhouettes down. I owed them some dignity. They all deserved my benevolent gaze before I slipped them back into the oblivion of their boxes. That they'd come into my hands was not a matter of choice but an accident. Still, it was for me to help them step into another life, no mat-ter that to them—wherever they were by now—my fervor didn't mean much anymore.

Then my eyes fell on a gait so unlike the others, one that reached me from a whole other story, even if, having come this far, I did not suspect that woman's silhouette could have once crossed my life.

{10}

About Choice

From all the gray people coming and going in varied settings and seasons—all trapped in an endless agony of winter—one stood out, bathed in a light unlike that of any of the other sequences, a woman with a slender figure, an accurate geometry for anyone who might take the time to look at her.

In the portion of film allotted to her, Stela was doing nothing other than walking. No more than three-quarters of her body showed on the screen. What she walked on remained a matter of guessing. But from her gait, her *disinvoltura*, one would imagine some mechanical device beneath her feet, perhaps a moving walkway, as in an airport. Focused on her movement, the camera had not provided context. A while ago, she had been carrying a large box, dangling from a half unhinged handle, not exactly a suitcase, but more of an obsolete apparatus. It slightly rounded her shoulders without upsetting her pace. But in the close-up, the hypnotic woman just moved on, as if relieved of the now invisible burden.

Why did that part of the film revolve in my mind more than the others when Stela herself was no longer on my mind? Was it the sudden shift from weight to lightness, some hinge that made her body shift beyond breaking? Or the attention she gave to each step, going to the bone of the movement with what appeared as inborn elegance, one that clashed with the disjointed chorus of the gloomy figures?

{11}

Our Temporary Residence

I am not a man of words and have remained as wary of a turn of phrase as I would be of the hairpin curve on a steep country road at night, which I find no less hazardous at any time of the day, regardless of one's caution or the speed of one's reflexes. Some might talk about a purpose of shape and color, a cellular affinity between the eye, the fingertips, and the viscous color spread on a canvas with knives of varied blade-widths. Or, they might describe thin vibrating blades on the grainy surface of the canvas that resonate in shades with no name. But that's not quite on my wavelength.

For me, things have been much simpler in the lean years of my nomad life: a torn shirt would do as a canvas that I'd paint on over and over. Sooner than you think, it turns into a habit, and, if I dare say, into a method: shapes break and recombine into large smooth surfaces in different color plots, the knife pats dark or luminous spots on the open surfaces, a gesture from one layer of paint is continued into another. But, as it happens, something else keeps me going, something that has neither shape nor color: simply, what remains of paint in the air when it's all finished, the eyes weary, the body limp: a translucent cloud of chemical vapors, a fume of poppies. The vapors make my head spin when the paint is still tacky, and then they hang there, get into my hair and skin, spread throughout the room. Turpentine: that's what drew me to my occupation.

Like me, Cora is fond of vapors. Turpentine is what's between her and me. She, too, likes the pungent residues of paint, even if they affect her rather badly. The studio is small. Vapors fill the air, overwhelm her nostrils, remind her of ether, and for a while benumb her sense of smell. I bring home bouquets of sweet basil, cloves in gauze pouches, I spread verbena-scented water on my neck. The fear that losing her sense of smell might affect Cora's warning system, her recollections, even perhaps her body's balance creeps into our nights.

She cannot sense the fragrance of herbs and spices now, but she does remember how she'd err in my garden passing her hands through the redolent shrubs, squeezing leaves between her fingers, patting her temples with their sap green tips. One day, Cora bursts into the studio with an armful of verbena, rushes to the kitchen cupboard, drops a few leaves in the teapot, pours hot water over them, and raises the glass pot to eye level, smiling as she did the day when I recalled that she was Stela's daughter:

"What's that color, Luca: stellar green?"

I draw a slow animal. A teapot. A caterpillar groping on the porous paper. But, to tell the truth, all I draw is Cora.

In my sleep, she is a fabled animal, but every morning I see her as she showed up in the improvised gallery. On the threshold she stood: a freshly finished portrait, a woman with a sprout-green scarf wrapped around her head, a few amber locks sticking out to frame her face.

{*12*}

Like that dog, she runs through my dark landscapes: the same alertness, the same trust.

{13}

Portrait (Black & White)

The rescued reels were black-and-white film, and by the time I got around to watching them, the film was sprinkled with flickers and dark spots, the woman's eyes the only source of light in that murky environment. In spite of the lack of color, there was something green about those eyes. Green kept coming back to me, at first without the faintest thought of Stela. I watched the film in a loop before I sat down to draw the figure, the woman's figure on the screen, tried to give a shape to the way she had of carrying her gaze over a space I couldn't see, then hiding her eyes, for a while, behind her sunglasses to prevent intrusion; tried in vain to sketch out the dignity and grace she radiated, one that some would pay to have, but which she seemed rather forced to hide.

It was that conspiracy of light I wanted to preserve on paper. A distinct green tone from the black-and-white film, as in glimmers of forest pools or sparkles of firework flowers. The full spectrum of colors came to my rescue. I mixed, painted in, over, and out. Some nebulous form was about to surface, layering space, turning limpid, light. It trotted at the corner of my eye like a slip of the tongue. But the exact tone of green I seemed to read in the eyes of the woman in the black-and-white film when she lifted her sunglasses over her forehead wouldn't come out right.

With time, the film altered critically and I had to stop thinking about color and the touch of a brush and just find a way to save it. The vinegar syndrome, I should have thought of it, and of how aging film grows increasingly dangerous, how nitrate film creates its own oxygen, and if it catches fire no water will put it out. So many stretches of life have been lost on account of that chain of chemical accidents. Thankfully, even after so long, the figures on my found reels kept breathing in their boxes, as best as they could, and I had to keep them breathing, keep them out of danger, keep the picture moving, but save that woman from reaching a dangerous point in her life.

How could I have missed it? The fugitive portrait I craved to make was already there, on the film, not in my sketchbook, nor in my color mixtures. The flickers and dark spots disappeared when it was restored, but her resilient strength endured all doctoring of the film, all relocation. I was attached to her unlike I'd ever been to any other woman, she who had slipped out of my mind as a one-time next-door neighbor who once gave me a bowl of rice pudding with cinnamon in remembrance of her father's death. For days, the warm print of her palms embracing that glass bowl rested within mine. That very woman, carrying on along a celluloid strip as shiny as a sheet of clear water, now looked at me from a place in myself I no longer knew how to reach.

Until, one day, a poet's lines resonated with that long forgotten memory: *water equals time & provides beauty with its double.*

{14}

A Man at the Bar

Outside our temporary residence we feel slightly adrift. It's not an unpleasant frame of mind. Cora and I have built up our routines. We walk, bike, explore the fields around us, stop to watch the light change on the surface of the ponds, nod to passersby, dig into abandoned farms in a seamless conversation with what we are at heart.

In the half-deserted village, my fellow artists and I are here to bring about some life, life of another kind, but still life: words nested on peeling walls; corridors expanded by neon lights; on the screen of an old television monitor, a slim figure; the debris of a car hanging from the mildewy beam in an empty barn, or what remains of it; and, in the backyard of what had once been a home, *papier maché* goblins cheering up visitors. The local pubs too have been rehabilitated. There, Cora and I expand our community of two. Local people, artists, and visitors get together at *In de Zon* or *De Blauwe Grens*, mainly. They drink, laugh, chat, and when they don't hit upon a common idiom, they move to sign language.

It was here that I chose to tell Cora my part of the story, something I couldn't, didn't want to contaminate our breathing room with. My part of the story, or what of it I happened to come across. When she was fifteen and her emotions were so close to the skin, there were things I had to hold back from her. She did have reasons to discard the accident story, of course, but the idea that Stela had defected and was someday, somehow going to take Cora out of the country seemed, even to my mind, suspect, hard to believe, and it was beyond question that Stela had abandoned her, as she had been inclined to believe since the day the news about Stela's death came to her ears. There were yet other possibilities I considered but could not have shared with her at that time, because of her age, the circumstances, because of my own doubts and fears of interfering with the course of the girl's life. So Cora's mind kept spinning as she sketched little figures on large-grain paper. Little figures moving up and down, left to right, up and down. And why wouldn't her mind spin and spin around an obscure axis if she hadn't herself seen Stela go. Unbelievable as the news was to everyone—as such news always is—for Cora the accident had simply not happened. It did not happen because she had not seen Stela in the sealed metal box that brought her home and, from there, after two days' wake, to the place of everlasting green. Cora was away on a tour with her dance group, her first, in a neighboring country. It was said that something had gone wrong with the telephones and telegrams; while she was on the road, some unpredictable conspiracy of incidents prevented the news from reaching her. So when she returned, one month after it had all happened, instead of Stela, a cortege of people, all dressed in black, met her at the train station.

I followed young Cora in her doubts about Stela's accident. She needed them to carry on with her life. Yet, for my part, I was rather inclined to explore the details in the official reports, compare them to what acquaintances had said. But who could help me? No one, for sure, the officials less than anyone else. Still, a number of nebulous details turned up in my mind, details that had to be kept away from the girl because they were unsettlingly vague and she was too young to grasp the shifting nature of truth. Why, for instance, after Stela's disappearance, did the postman, passing their house, peer through the lattice gate, mumbling, "Not many letters lately, none from abroad"? Or, why, some years before the accident, did Stela suddenly look changed, her complexion the color of clay, her pace slower than it had ever been when I'd watch her pass by my house with a pile of books in her hands, or a bag of rations? And why, when I dared speak to her, to ask "How are you," to say, "Haven't seen you in a while," did she look over her shoulder, then back at me, her lips sketching an embarrassed smile as she searched for the right word, one that she, a doctor's assistant, must have been quite familiar with: "Oh, he-pa-ti-tis." "In the hospital," she whispered, "for twenty years." And although it was, no doubt, "weeks" she meant (as far as I'd heard, that's how long she'd been away), her absent air, her vacant gaze, made that lapse of time, indeed, potentially expand to so many years. Twenty weeks for trying to pass a letter to a foreign official visiting our homeland, Cora had found out or assumed from bits and pieces she had managed to gather or came across.

At the bar, a man stands by Cora's side. Dressed in a tweed jacket that makes him look uncomfortable, he puffs smoke through his nostrils and wipes the angle of the counter back and forth, back and forth. Somehow out of place, this man, comic with a tragic twist at the corners of his mouth, reminds me of another, the man I had once suspected of being the anonymous driver of the red car that collided with Stela, but, as it turned out, was not. A man I met over a glass or more of beer, shortly after I'd left the country, when the girl and her mother still lingered in my mind. He had owned a red car once, that man I met, and carried some kind of guilt with him. He was a draftsman in an obscure office, or so he said, but in another life he might as well have been a private eye, more of a lone wolf than a plainclothes man, like those who'd paved the paths of my youth with good intentions. Unbidden, many glasses later, he unreeled a story he must have rarely, if ever, let out.

Wouldn't he have noticed the woman on the berm of the road leading to the border river, even when it was too late to brake?

No, he swore to God, on the light of his eyes.

He had not seen her before (or after) the impact.

Nor had he heard her body fall, though the thud must have reverberated from the asphalt through the open window of his rushing car. The bump, yes, he felt it in his stomach as he picked up even more speed and the asphalt vibrated under the wheels of the car and to the top of his head. That shock, the bump into what feels like inert matter even before the fall, he had it under his skin to this day.

He dashed down the road then and onto the highway.

And for whoever wants to hear what it was all about, he said rather unnervingly, fear, yes, that's all there was. Not fear of the consequences of the impact (in that speeding moment, he insisted, he was still unaware it had been a woman he'd hit) but fear of his own inert body, and he'd been running from that accident inside ever since, running away from himself well after he got out of jail (he did, eventually, do a stint, but later, and for something that happened on another road), and, perhaps, to the end of his days.

But he was positive: that woman—the one he did not have the time to see—had no daughter.

Because he did have a chance to look for her later, or he'd given himself that chance. He found her name in the paper the day after the accident, before he crossed the border. She was a local woman, said a minor news item lost among photographs of flags, military parades, and wooden-leg sentences. She was caught up, it seemed, in an argument with a man who had long since vanished. She'd dashed across the street to escape his grip. The woman was herself a loner, someone who pretended to have witnessed the accident told him, or she was known as such in that small border town where this man I'd met later returned, drawn by remorse or just curiosity, for his life was, after all, tied to hers, wasn't it? She had no family, no relatives, no one to mourn her, no one who might remember what she was like or even that there had been an accident on that particular day on the road to the border river. It was a busy road, and there had been so many.

When I come to the end of my story, or part of it, I hear Cora drawl:

"Red cars come in numbers, you know."

And then the knot in her voice seems to have melted, only her hand vibrates vaguely on the bar's flat surface:

"In principle, I understand there's need for justice to have its say. But would it matter to me now, or at any other time, if he had been judged or if he hadn't? Suppose he'd been caught right after he ran out of the accident zone: would that have changed anything for me? And what if someone thought there was no need to catch him, if he'd just followed an order?

"And what do we know? Perhaps it wasn't a car that took Mother away." Her voice raised, her hands quivering:

"Why bring this up, Luca? Leave the man alone. I have work to do."

Suite for Two

Cora, I have known two of her: the teenager and the woman. And though her stage name—Aura Stern—has a familiar resonance, it also points to a hazy elsewhere, where we all come from. But for me she'll always be Cora, and I love the touch of the two syllables on my lips, they resonate with a crisp day in September when the skinny girl knocked at my door, a bunch of drawings under her arm. When her ear brushes her shoulder and—hands parted, head back, eyes closed—she rotates around her spine with a suspension of direction and a speed that makes her body grow thinner and thinner, I've got to catch her hip with one hand, grasp an elbow, hold a wrist in my palm to keep her from flying away. She says Cora's a name she never really liked, but she doesn't mind my calling her that in private. She's Aura Stern now: a name for two. A *watermark*. Yes, in a certain light, the resemblance is striking.

Who else but Cora and I would care about the color of Stela's eyes?

In the absence of anyone even slightly familiar with what's passed in the old country, it is left to me to rehearse all the spectrum of remembrance I can into her orphaned ear. I who crossed paths with Cora's mother only a couple of times.

While I pat the canvas with the thin blades, try consistencies of paint on a tile, Cora trains her body, practices her routines to exhaustion, then brings her breath back to an even pace. I watch her count to eight in sleep, defy gravity, spend her waking hours reshaping the space we share. I spy on her as she performs a whole repertory of gestures: handling flowers in a vase, bringing their colors into a provisional agreement, shifting the set, creating still and moving lives that help her pass from one day to another in our temporary residence. She has her way of going about it: innate, unaffected, necessary. Each gesture—true, stripped to the bone—carries its own beauty, brings a transitory resolution to a loss. Something happens, or might happen. Day after day, her improvisations bring some kind of order into the mayhem of our lives, or maybe it's surprise. She draws her strength from these domestic choreographies.

Loose-wristed, drooping hand, half-rounded arm, lifting leg, vibrating foot. Her moves are as clear as light after a storm. Still, something seems to hold her back: each gesture carves the air as it should, yet they don't connect, they don't flow, not always. Something lacks focus or doesn't quite fit into her mental script, an inner gesture, perhaps, something that's not quite hers. There is a small gap, or a shimmer, that prompts conflicting signs. Her limbs, neck, and spine dwell in confusion, for a moment.

Then an arm sends rapid signals into the air.

The fingers follow suit.

The arm proliferates, it unfolds a satin strip.

I catch sight of the hallucination she kindles with her chang-

ing steps: a gait I can tell from any other, Stela's silhouette flickering in and out with a swish. It pulls, falls, rises, gives her a gesture
to develop. Aura catches it. And I can tell my part is over: she's
reached something she alone can reach, since the figure Aura
spins out of her body is not part of me as she is of her.

I can still see a place in the night where she stood. Caught in
a circle of soft light.

Her beauty dwelled in that blur.

{16}

Summer & Mail

It's reached us, at last, the letter she's been waiting for as she kept practicing her steps, developing her endurance, her body's capacity for surprise. The dance company she applied to work with before our paths crossed again is now welcoming her. They are the right people. They move like she moves, and Cora's wait for them to put their faith in her has turned out to be worthwhile, as I had no doubt it would. Others might appreciate her capabilities, of course, but they wouldn't know how to use her. She doesn't quite fit in, is not exactly what the public wants. Cora doesn't mind (or so she says). She has to find out how to bring that awkward and persistent body in tune with others. What I did not—could not—tell her was that the company might turn out to be just another illusion, vital, no doubt, but no substitute for what she'd lost. Yet, what else could she do? She had to go her way, and try as I might, I'll never be enough company for her.

We walk in the orchard of what was a home to someone once, not far from where I placed the video piece that had brought us into unhoped-for complicity. A lazy wind brushes the acacia branches, and the fabric of light they print on the ground keeps us caught in a space of subdued apprehension. As we move, the branches stay quiet and a faint voice comes from above, followed by others, all speaking out in slightly varied rhythms what seems to be the same sequence, or part of a sequence. We pass by the pond shimmering with colored syllables, and then we come to a chestnut tree, embrace it, holding each others' hands tightly, and turn around it, our heads tilted back, oscillating around the spiraling center of the tree crowns. She murmurs something that makes little sense to me, directions that nevertheless seem to fit the scene:

have them turn around a chestnut tree

Heads revolving, bodies flashing like a thunderbolt, we turn and turn as she had planned, while the sky spins and the grass holds our feet to the ground.

Take your body and go, the branches whisper.

Take your body and go, softly, softly, until the syllables evaporate into the late afternoon and the electric blue arch above our heads slows its twirling.

"I've heard that voice before," Cora says, the top of her index finger to her lips, "I've, heard it," she says, eyes half closed, "in the true and not uncommon story of a simple woman, Anita. Vanished: she, her man, the baby boy, and the daughter. Twenty years she spent away, far away: twenty years in Siberia. It is a story she wrote down, I heard, on her return. Because, eventually, she did return, close to the end of her life, to a home that was no longer hers, but welcomed her nonetheless. She returned because times had changed or, thanks to her brother, whom a twist of fate had pushed onto another road, one which—unlike hers—led to a destination outside of the perimeter of fear. For twenty years he'd been working her way out of the wilderness with petitions or letters to foreign officials. For many like him, it was the only thing they could do: pass the letter from hand to hand, from the provinces to the capital and hope to find a helpful hand, like Stela's.

"Anita had no time to lock her door, no time to say good-bye. If anything, it was the crop she thought of, the acres left unharvested, and, yes, the baby, not yet six months old and not baptized, an ill omen, even more so when one is forced to take the unhallowed child on a journey without end, struggle for air, water, a crumb now and then.

"Someone in the distance shouted: 'They're coming. No time to pack. Run!' And yes, there was no more time, the commotion of heavy iron was getting closer, and at once the ground rattled right there under their feet. The wind brought the rumble of tanks and trucks, mixed with dust, insults, vile laughter, smashed bottles. Her brother shouted something from a place she couldn't see. And then something went awry: the horse, the wheel, the road, the dust? The path forked and, when the cloud of dust settled into a thin film on the mud, they were all alone on the wrong road: she, her man, the baby boy, the daughter. When the soldiers came to snatch them (she and the baby and the girl—her man she'd never see again), she thought, 'Who'll take care of the horse, now?' and 'What will become of Mother, abandoned in the house?' She just scribbled a note for the neighbors, in case it reached them, to take care of her, and dropped it on the road. Because she had no time for more. There they were, the soldiers: young, red in the face, dressed in ashy telogreikas, craving golden coins and watches. They pushed her and the children into a truck, barking brutal words with bent vowels. They laughed. They spit. They slammed the truck door in their faces.

"Years later, many landscapes away, all gray and bone dry, Anita was really in a bad way. She was brought to a makeshift hospital. She passed out. Nearly comatose, she prayed to get well, to get back to her children, even to their new home, their cold home in the wilderness. And just as she woke, she heard someone speak to her:

you want so bad to go back to your children
and then another:
you'll be released, take your body and go
ia-ti corpul si du-te

"But how could she take her body? How could she tell her body from the others—there were so many lying around and they all looked the same? Then she thought of the lump she had on her left hand. It had gotten bigger with all the work she had been forced to do, or perhaps it grew because of the cold. By then it was as big as a chicken's egg. She felt so lucky for that lump.

"I've had that woman with me for a while," Cora says. "She comes and goes.

"There were many like her.

"How many?"

Cora looks back at the old house, at me, and then, as we walk away through the orchard, she breaks a young branch from a wild apple tree and makes a wreath of it in one go. I carry her in my arms, with a slight embarrassment for my clumsiness, for she is heavier than she looks. As we cross the threshold of our shared home, I put her back on her feet. There isn't much else I can do. She moves about the four corners of the studio in haste, glances out the window, brushes my neck with her fresh breath, then stuffs her clothes in a bag. She puts on her black-cherry velvet jeans, her soft leather sandals, and a purple shirt. Some noise distracts me, a bird out there, or the telephone, and when I turn my gaze back I notice a handful of loose, red amber beads she had one day dropped in a shell on my desk. The corners of her lips rise into a smile, she moves her ring to her middle finger—a quick note of something she had to think of—turns her green scarf twice around her head, and tiptoes toward the door on her heels instead of the balls of her feet, and very swiftly at that, in a thrilling way that makes the floor vibrate. The whole room is roused by her sudden haste. I empty the beads into my palm, but by the time I've grabbed a napkin to pack them in, the door has opened and shut smoothly. Her pace on the wooden stairs sounds light yet determined. I drop the beads into the bowl. There is no point in adding more weight to her shoulders.

She has a long way to go.

It rains all night. Heavy, streaming, clear rain.

What kind of steps would she make out of the pattering on the roof, I wonder. Then sleep takes me out for a walk in the wet, tepid night. The rain slackens. The streets seem safe and quiet. The Weimaraner sits in front of a closed gate. It has by now stopped fighting with the dust. I should call him by his name, but instead of the name, a white cloud comes out of my mouth, soft, rounded, and thick as only sleep can fabricate, spiraling then into a long whistle.

"There are still steps I cannot match, you know," the dog says, in a poised voice. "Some combinations I miss. But never mind! I don't hold it against you. After all, it's none of your fault. Sit down and have a drink with me. Say, haven't seen you around in a while."

I pat him on his back. His coat is soft as cashmere. He must have cleaned it for the occasion.

"Have you got your passport yet?" I mean to ask, but am not quite sure what language to use.

A silvery car pulls up and stops beside us, spattering the edge of my trench coat with mud. The dripping orange letters on its door read: "Apolodor T_xis". The ride will save me getting drenched.

I hop in and wave to the dog, as one does in situations like this, holding, instead of a handkerchief, a crumpled piece of paper in my right hand.

By now, Cora must have caught her train.

Run my dog—run—a hostage to the night—I pray for you.

THE DREAM SOLUTION

{1}

Water & Salt

Clear seawater is heavier than turbid freshwater because salt is heavier than earth.

Day after day, I train my body to overcome its weight. Everything I own is stored in there. All over, from the root of my hair to the white moons of my toenails. I carry my body and my body carries me. We operate on trust and I've trained it to recall—counting from one to eight—which of its parts does what, from where, and how each movement comes about. Out of the blue, some dormant gesture in a tissue, some glint in a stretched muscle shows me the way, puts me on another track. Odds and ends revolve around a nerve. They shift my moves, affect my balance. Balls of thread unwind. Ribbons pop out of my fingers. Then they stop short. I count to eight and carry on. They don't.

Something fails me and I'm not quite sure what. Whether it is small or large, close or remote, solid or loose, heavy or light. Whatever it is, I take the weight out of it. I do my best. I turn the air over, slice it, hold on, undo the shape of one arm, pass it to the next. I grope as far as I can reach.

Because that's all there is.

Over time, I have acquired the craft of keeping still between one move and another. Suspended. It is a matter of technique that calls for practice, perseverance, a set of procedures and a degree of inadvertence. But for how long, for how long can I carry on holding onto nothing but air?

On the road, where I have been more than once, I have designed my own chart of movements and steps day by day: curve, tilt, twist. And, at every station the train passes by or stops at, Stela keeps coming back while I improvise fugitive choreographies in my mind. They ask for little room other than what's in there: space after space after space. I rehearse the scripts with my eyes closed, or as I watch the passing landscape, in the rhythm of a song Stela'd murmur like a prayer to sustain me through the night:

> *Ich geh' mit meiner Laterne*
> *und meine Laterne mit mir.*
> *Da oben leuchten die Sterne*
> *und unten, da leuchten wir.*
> *Laternlicht,*
> *verlösch mir nicht!*
> *Rabimmel, rabammel, rabum*

{2}

Summer & Mail

Here is a letter Luca doesn't know about, a letter of another kind than the one I've been expecting. Instead of the creepy postman who'd killed my dog, a middle-aged messenger dressed in a dark suit with well-worn sleeves and an off-white silk scarf around his neck hands it to me (or is about to). His nails are neatly trimmed, in contrast with the skin of his hands, burned by the sun, like old leather. In spite of the blue-purple circles around his eyes, he looks impeccable, graceful: the kind of man who comes from old movies, or old somewheres, a figure who stands out in any sort of light. You can tell one from a distance, there aren't many of them left. ("Men in wan gray or blue overalls and uniforms all over the place, no proper language, no manners," as Grandmother pointed out, with good reason, when she saw men and women go about their nonsense duties, unnervingly indolent, men and women who, for one reason or another, agreed to live on hate, ignorance, indoctrination. Yes, Grandmother would have liked this man who seems to have come a long way to bring a letter to me. Their paths might have crossed somewhere long ago, or maybe he just looks like Grandfather used to in his good days.)

Regardless of the men in wan overalls and uniforms, and in spite of the warm weather, my bearer of news won't part with his black felt hat, except to greet me courteously with a slight bow. His well-groomed words flow smoothly, and he gives each one the attention he seems to deem it deserves.

"If you prefer, young lady," he says, "I can read the note to you. No peccadillo. I am conversant with such things, if I may have your trust. I make a living out of it. That's all there is left for me to do."

I stare at him, then look over my shoulder, drop my arms, make him understand that that's all right with me. Peccadillo! Not the kind of word in use these days, but quite in tune with his outfit, his gestures. He clears his voice and starts reading the letter with commitment to his mission, but gently and in an almost playful way, as if each word were a ball he tossed from one palm to the other with skill and nonchalance. His eyes follow the felt balls and, now and then, he checks on me, for a split second, as his words (or whoever's they are) roll down my shoulders:

The infinite space between heaven and earth is called air.
Air is not the ethereal substance that envelops the earth but simply
space. Space that has been randomly partitioned into several zones,
separated by barbed wire and watched over by tollhouse collectors.
They hold out against the soul's progress to its destination.
You are to pass the customs in this world here—there is that
letter to hand over.
Someone's life hangs on it.

Then he rounds his lips as if to blow a kiss, or puff out a thick silver cloud from a cigar, and hums what seems to be his own gloss to that strange pronouncement, or perhaps he's just trying to alleviate the dry heat blurring the contours of the trees across the street:

> *"Leni murmure candidum*
> *Audisses Zephyrum tibi*
>
> *aethere*

There should be a proper ritual, if I may suggest."

Such a smart-looking man, such nonsense.

Postmen make me uneasy. In fact, they turn my stomach. Just seeing one knock or ring at others' doors on pretty days without the shadow of an omen gives me a rash. And no matter how much he seems to care, even this man of another make than the obnoxious postmen of my younger days, even this considerate, well-read man brings me to the brim of a dizzy spell, spells that pass as they have come: a crimson ring clasps my temples, a wave scoops my stomach, the ground slides under my feet, like a moving walkway in a stifling underground corridor. I am about to pass out. But I don't. Firm on my feet, I manage to articulate my doubt, good manners notwithstanding:

"What do I have to do with that letter, sir?"

He doesn't seem offended by my question nor by my tone. In his quiet manner, he bows halfway, walks to the gate, comes back, puts his hand in his right pocket, brings it out empty. Then, changing his mind again, he returns to the gate and steps out, leaving me in silence. As he walks out of my sleep, I hear him say as to himself: "Once, such words would have put my life (or even yours) at risk. Godspeed, young lady. Take care of yourself. We'll be expecting news from you."

What was it about that letter, whose contents only he could understand, that turned my thoughts to Stela?

Never mind that she herself may not have been carrying a letter with her the day she vanished.

And who told me there was one to begin with?

Did anyone ever mention it?

Have I made it up?

Who knows?

It's been so long.

Yes, it's been quite a while now. All I know for certain is that I came home and there was no more Mother, no more Domenica.

Everyone does the best they can.

Grandmother's tears dried while she waited for me to get home and grow up.

The dog kept turning over the earth in the flowerbeds for a while, then wailed her way out of our lives, or what was left of them.

Lately, I have come to terms with the fact that it is not within my means to evaluate the situation.

I've mostly been busy strengthening my muscles and trying out new steps, testing how far they can bring me, how much they can help me unbind old knots.

It is impossible at one and the same time that the mover should move the movable object and the movable object its mover.

{3}

Fluctuation Zone

One day I pass a border for the first time ever, though I'm not an adult yet. I travel with my dance group with a permit and return ticket. Stela makes a cake for me. A minced cherrystone cake topped with lemon meringue, wrapped up in a white cotton napkin sprinkled with field flowers at the corners, Grandmother's meticulous needlework.

On the platform, Stela mimes instructions for me to follow: one palm flat below her chin, a hand raised to the mouth for "Do–not–drop–crumbs!"

The train is about to leave. She unknots her scarf to wave good-bye, then lets it loose. Or does the wind snatch it from her hand? The train sets off. And when she is no more than a dancing spot fading away, the scarf has taken on a life of its own. It throbs, ripples, swells.

Through the departing train's long-unwashed window, a thick, gray-brownish crowd is all I can see other than the pale iris scarf that slows its pace and breath above the electric poles, then hangs there, watching over the rails. After a while, its color has bleached out. Only its scent persists: soap, clear water, milk.

What if I never see Mother again?

At the border, the customs militiamen check papers, search my pockets, my bag, the lining of my coat. A routine like any other, and a thorough one at that. The cake is all that's left to be inspected. Who knows, there might be something hidden inside, some small nothing, some cypher a teenager like me, of unhealthy roots, would carry abroad. The cake must be cut. Be-head-ed! The men in uniform seem to be as puzzled by the presence of a cake in my bag as I am by their request to have it hacked to pieces. They do me a favor, no matter how rude they look, and hand me a greasy knife so that I may do it myself. I don't. They'll have to put their heavy hands on it but there is dirt under their nails. Dried blood. I shout, frantically gesticulate, and save my cake, still young enough to take a stand. And do I know there'll never be another cake made by Mother?

In time, I have gotten used to crossing borders with nothing to declare, nothing more than what no one would care about. Except that now I have Luca to remember. Luca who did remember Stela even as she had slipped out of his mind. And in that place where he and his friends made what it was their job to make and brought life back into an abandoned village, he'd worked out a solution for those rescued reels, and Mother found her way again into so many eyes. What did it matter that on those two black-and-white screens she remained nameless?

The old customhouse stands idle in the midst of rampant weeds. Run-down and idle, the custom guards' booth shares its boredom with a hotel in the distance, equally abandoned and despondent.

From now on, the frontier—as signposts dressed in black plastic hoods advise—shall be called *a zone of fluctuating disposition.* The checkpoints have become redundant. Inspections are performed on random travelers only. Rules concerning who should be checked and why are more unpredictable in this new environment, since, unlike stepping on snow, walking in chaos conceals fugitive footprints.

At all events, if a customs guard happens to stop me, I will reply serenely that I know well what I have done and why. I need to keep my head above suspicion without deviating from my codes. If a comma drops from my pocket, I will bend down and pick it up, put it back where it belonged. No one can confiscate it, nor divert me from the road I have chosen. Dangerous words are not my habit. Mother taught me to keep such words at bay, and I've been practicing what I saw at home: silence, sighs, and shrugs. A secret alphabet, the work of hands and gazes.

I am too tall and mostly awkward, but I know how to pass, kick, fall, and run.

I dance about things that happen.

And one day Luca turned up from nowhere. Was I still thinking of him as I passed border after border to save my life and, with it, Stela's? Did any remnant of the handsome young man, my salutary neighbor, persist in me? Not as a distinct figure, perhaps, but more of an opaque sweeping silhouette or substance, a companion to those I have been carrying along with me, by day or by night.

Sometimes, I am myself an idle border.

{4}

Moni, Laika, and I

In our backyard there was a doghouse where I would hide when I hadn't held my tongue. The length of my stay there depended on the kind of story I'd come up with, a story whose real consequences were, in fact, impossible for me to imagine.

If truth be told, I didn't really make up these stories, I just rehearsed my repertoire of observations. I absorbed as much as I could, picked up trifles here and there from whispers and murmurs, a name or a word whose implications I would ignore, a stray detail from a lost conversation, odds and ends I would then fit into some tall tale, which, to my simple mind, was worth passing around. Child stuff, antics, all above suspicion, at least as far as I could see. Mother and I differed with regard to that, though she never told me not to shout over the neighbors' fences the words and names I'd heard her and Grandmother let out, not to mention them in class, not to tell stories I made out of them, never ever, not even in our house. She never spoke about danger, expressly I mean.

"You have too much tongue," is all she said.

Or:

"That's not true. You'd better do your homework, and your routines, Miss."

She was right. I just enjoyed chattering whenever I had a chance, and, most of all, I enjoyed figuring out what the grown-ups were plotting behind my back. I had to fill in the gaps because I missed most of it, and, honestly, I suspected all that whispering was about me. It stands to reason that I would exaggerate, edit, embellish. But that was Mother: she didn't like too much lip. Or, rather, she mistrusted it. She got that from her family, I have come to think. Because there had been one before there was none. An unyielding family, outspoken, faithful to their simple rules. Grandfather above all. No tongue in his pockets. No lip service.

"You'll pay for it," some said; others implied it with a glance or a gesture.

And we have. At the time I knew nothing about the power of hate, envy, manipulation, but I still had a hunch that those simple rules, the family's candid faith in them threatened our lives: theirs, and through a chain of unpredictable consequences following a word dropped against us here and there, mine, as well.

Soon I learned the art of silence.

Forgetting comes with it. Or so you think.

Mother knew better.

At any rate, when I was about to turn seven I had other things to care about. And I didn't hold it against Mother that I had to hide in the doghouse for shame, or guilt, or just for fun. I've always felt at home with animals, of the same make, the same energy. I didn't mind the thick layers of dog hair on that shelter's floor. We both sat or curled up on it, our warm mattress.

The insides of bodies Mother sketched for the medical school exam on thin, crisp, transparent paper came to mind when I closed my eyes. She didn't have much time to play with me, or she didn't like to, or she was just too burdened with distress, but sometimes she'd draw me close and show me how bodies work. Grandmother peeked at us through the doorway. She, too, would have liked to step into the secret space Mother and I shared, to understand how bodies worked, where the world was going, and so on. Anyway, she didn't miss much, because to me, it wasn't really bodies that Stela and I looked at, but red and green lines, some thicker, some thinner, more like a mind-boggling system of wires.

"Bundles of nerves and muscle fibers is what we are made of," she said, reading my mind as she so often did.

And then, taking my head in her hands:

"What you see here is all over your small body, it goes through your hands, toes, neck, skull, here, yes, all the way in here." And she kissed me on my forehead.

When we looked closer, white spaces surfaced between the bundles. She pointed to one: "An interstice." That's what she called it. And no matter how hard it was to pronounce, the word sounded to me very much like where I'd take refuge if I didn't follow her instructions about good manners and behavior: in the dog's house, an in-ter-tice of sorts, where I'd find refuge!

"No," Stela corrected me, "in-ter-*s*tice."

I liked it there, though, in the dog's house, the air made warm by the dog's breath, by his comforting body. The night smelled of burnt cloth. The dog and I were fine, our shelter a capsule for the two of us, perfect for clandestine journeys that could expand our lives. In there, the dog and I were going all the way around the world and then even farther onto the most remote galaxies.

Moni and I were going to beat Laika's triumph over space, gravity, tollhouses.

But then summer ended. In winter, we were in holding pattern. Weather conditions in a country that has the shape of a flat fish can be hostile to such experiments, we were told at an early age. Weather conditions and any ideas related to alien environments made traveling dangerous. Still, rocking there in our capsule, Moni and I pursued our secret plans, while I conjugated the forms of silence, wondering whether Laika had ever made it back to earth or, if she hadn't, what became of the small, warm, throbbing body out there in cold space.

When Moni was poisoned by unknown hands, we dug a hole in the front yard. Milk didn't help. Mother said milk is not good against poison. She ran into the house to get something. As she hurried down the steps, carrying whatever it was, before she even touched him, Moni opened his mouth. Then he closed it.

We dug a hole in the flowerbeds.

It was all we could do for him.

Laika, I learned long after she was gone, didn't survive for even seven hours orbiting the earth alone in her flying box. It took years for the capsule to dissolve in space.

Which one had a better chance?

{5}

Grundig

Me and Missus Jones I played on Saturdays, *Missus Jones, Missus Jones, Missus Jones! Oh, Lord, won't you buy me a Mercedes Benz*, and *Summertime* on Sundays. The other days I went to school. Not something I was much inclined to do, but I had to please Grandmother, and Mother would have objected to my being idle, wouldn't she?

The next-door neighbor passed that tape to me, the only one I ever had.

He had a tan complexion, a fine nose, curly hair running down his neck. I fancied him, as they say, but, a shy teenager, I didn't know much about men. ("You should be wary of them," Mother said.)

He stopped me by the gate, the suave neighbor. He tried to comfort me without indulging in conventions. He spoke of Stela's beauty, paintings, pictures; of the cloud above our house, of spring. I suspected he had skills in staying alive.

One day, I put on a better dress, tied my hair in a ponytail, picked up my courage and knocked at his door, my notebooks with stick figures under my arm. I'd been thinking of a cool first line for days, but I missed the work of words. Luca's garden was full of mint, verbena, and weeds. He had many friends, friends his age. They smoked. They sang. They danced and did other things people their age do, I suppose. And they whispered a lot, at various frequencies, some in languages I didn't understand. In our house, I'd grown up with whispers, thought they had to do with some wrong I had done. But with Luca and his friends whispering seemed stylish. They did it with incredible ease, not an inkling of fear. Whispering spread out in his garden like a spider's web, like a shared secret life: a life elsewhere. It expanded from the garden, farther and farther, and connected to other gardens and homes filled with low voices, swinging murmurs, mingled with radio frequencies humming into the night.

"There's feeling in your drawings," Luca mumbled with a cigarette in the corner of his mouth as he looked at my sketchbook.

"They seem to occupy you, your little figures. Keep on drawing, but remember to smudge them at the corners."

Luca spoke like someone who knew what he was talking about. I did continue, smudging the figures' contours, if that was what he meant, until only clouds of crayon remained on the page, but I never showed them again, to Luca or anyone else, even if I still follow their pace when I rehearse: they are still my secret company.

In college I was slow, too slow. Dumb is how I felt, and I mostly just stumbled around in gym class. Too tall, too thin, a stick figure myself—the boys made fun of me. They shouted: "Get off the horse!" when I came close to the school gate. One more reason not to go to school. Another was feeling that my brain was being stuffed with fake matter, matter and words of another kind than what I was being fed at home. Wouldn't it have been better to stand up, raise my voice, and tell them that I do things they couldn't even imagine: ballet, piano, languages? Some languages I already spoke at home, or used to, with Mother, when we'd ride the tram downtown for this or that, and no one would make sense of our chattering. But I didn't raise my voice. It was better not to. Mother said I shouldn't speak of ballet, piano, or languages at school. Ever.

"Languages are not good," she said.

I never asked why she had me learn them if they weren't good. That was the way it was. Mother just knew best.

When I think of it, I haven't had measles, or mumps, or chicken pox. Mother kept me away from all that, protected me from contagion as well as she could. But, every once in a while, I came down with a spell of rage. It had to do with the wisdom teeth, I think, or who knew what. Other forms of contagion, of words, ideas, taste, seemed more delicate to fight against. Yet Mother had a way with them, too. There were so many things Mother knew better than I. Sometimes she'd risk a phrase in one language or another, and that was a message for the right thing to do. Of course, under the circumstances they were dangerous, those languages, as I eventually came to realize. But they did help me out of contagious spaces.

Mother's clothes were still in the closet, washed, ironed, and folded, made of rare fabrics: silk of many textures, bouclé, jersey, batiste, serge. I'd try them on every Sunday afternoon. Cream, indigo, mauve. Each piece with its own rustle, its own syllable at the tip of my fingers.

I talked to the neighbor in a whisper because I understood that's what one does. He thought I had good reasons not to believe the story about Mother's accident. He did his best to help. I knew he would.

There were days when I wasn't that dumb and I managed by myself. I could make good use of my brain, try to sort things out about Mother's being away, about possibilities of getting in touch with her. But I still had to go to school to sort out my own life.

"Life takes over," older people sermonized. They brought so little comfort that running away from home was the first wish on my list of Christmas presents to myself. Someday I'd do what Luca eventually did: defect. The word pattered on my lips. In English, above all, there was a sense of awe in it. I'd heard it on the radio, late at night, when I was hoping to hear news from Luca on short waves. It seemed natural to hold it against him, leaving me behind, but I couldn't. One day, who knows, I might even forget his name.

One of these mornings you're gonna rise up singing
And you'll spread your wings and you'll take to the sky

An orange plastic dwarf with a box of cigarettes in his hands grinned at me from one corner of the piano. I took a diminutive cigarette out of the box, stuck it in his crooked mouth, and lit it. The smoke smelled like incense. I sneezed him away. What was that gaudy dwarf doing there on our piano? He didn't have anything to do with Mother. He rolled across the floor. The cigarette dropped from his mouth, but he kept grinning. Plastic you can neither tear apart nor smash. And that's too bad.

In the dark living room, on Sunday mornings, I'd practice fall-ing with style. Loosen, fold, drop. It gave me pleasure to see that I could do it pretty well. With time and perseverance, I increased my vocabulary of moves. I could roll and crawl and rise. With one knee folded, I would use the strength of my other elbow to push myself up, as if I were climbing a high wall. In time, the wall got smaller and smaller, or perhaps my legs got longer. And then, over and over: loosen, fold, and phom! That's what I liked best. The thud and the fresh, sweet fragrance of the wooden floor. When I'd done well, it felt like an accomplishment: my signature of sorts. On Sundays, no one cared if I was too tall or clumsy. Rolling and crawling felt smooth as cream. The parquet shined. It smelled of honey. Grandmother waxed it every other week with a devotion reminiscent of an archaic ritual. Everything was clean and orderly in our house. We had so much room. So much room just for the two of us, Grandmother, who spent most of her time in the kitchen or in the garden, and me, getting out of the house as soon as I could.

Clean and orderly. No one even bothered us about the Grundig tape recorder anymore. Someone from an office at the district police station just called about the typewriter once in a while. But that had nothing to do with their suspicions con-cerning Mother, because I also learned how to use it. Of course, at that point, long after the accident, the militia or officers or plainclothes men might not even remember that I was Stela's daughter. But didn't they have that in their papers, over there, in the offices where we went to let them perform the typewrit-er's checkup? Everything was stored over there, many people implied. Was that really possible?

Eventually, they stopped calling. One of their men would just come to the house and invite me to bring the typewriter to the police station and, if I brought up the weight argument, he obligingly carried it for me. One of them, an older district militiaman, remembered Mother:

"Too bad," he kept mumbling as I dragged myself behind him. "Too bad. Too bad she was stubborn. I mean, she was a nice woman after all. Too bad."

Grandmother was so hard to read. Neither sorrow nor joy glimmered in her eyes, nothing but round mineral green. Just look her straight in the eyes and you'd lose ground. Mother I could cheer up with the handful of tricks in my pockets. But Grandmother was hard to please. So hard. We spent days and nights each of us on her ocean of silence. Every now and then, her expression softened as if she was about to reach a shaft of light, a cornflower in a meadow, a horse playing in his paddock. We'd go out, she'd buy me a steaming Greek cheese pie from the stand at the end of the street, or a necklace from the department store downtown. However, most of the time she kept herself busy with the house.

One day she declared that the time had come for me to wear a precious ring.

"But where would I buy one for you, now? We can't find rings like we used to have . . . ," she said.

(" . . . and have had to sell," she didn't say, but that's what I'd heard. I'd heard they sold all the precious things they had to feed me after father made another life for himself and Grandpa lost the life he'd been left with. That one and only ring was made of leftovers: bits of golden chain, orphan earrings, broken bracelets, tiny baptism crosses stripped of their necklaces. Whatever she couldn't sell under the table Grandmother had the goldsmith melt and shape into a golden band: the last ring Mother wore would now be mine, since there was no way to find a precious ring for me, one that suited Grandmother's taste.)

We went to the movies once in a while, Maia (my name for Grandmother) and I, when there was something worth seeing at the cinema round the corner. If we felt like it, we stayed on and watched the movie again, nobody cared. We saw *Mondocane*, *Yo-yo*, *Spartacus*. The movie house smelled of DDT. I know Maia would have gone more often to the movies if there were more worth seeing, but she never said so. Before times had changed, when streets had other names and people other faces, she used to seek refuge from her domestic tasks in movie houses downtown with their plush seats and gilded moldings. She wore light flowered dresses then, organdy, crepe georgette. On special occasions she'd put on a felt hat or a long string of dark red amber beads reaching down to her waist, held by a flowered box clasp that left a skin-deep imprint at the root of her neck. She patted satin powder on her face with a crimson velvet pad, and her lipstick came from a tin box that smelled of patchouli.

I'd always known Grandmother as old, though she never seemed so. Every six months a tight perm put new waves in her hair. In the interim she tended to grief and the bills. Maia didn't make much of my falling tricks. Rather, she worried that I might damage the oak parquet with its jazzy pattern, while I argued that the floor's contact with my body would rather increase its shine. In the end, she didn't seem to mind, so long as I had something to do that kept me from running away from home.

Maia on my bicycle, one bright Sunday. She keeps her balance. Laughs. Her laughter rolls along with the wheels. The sun brightens her face. I have never seen her laughing other than in photos, in her Sunday dresses, long ago. We could both run away, it occurs to me as I see her face shining, if we just had two bicycles. I would buy her a new powder pad, if I could find a nice one in a store, help her string the amber beads from the necklace that have survived over the years, survived the searches, the barter and the cash. But where would she go out now to wear an old amber necklace and a felt hat?

Mother had bought it from someone—the Grundig that had been "smuggled into the country," someone reported, spelling out something like a secret code: "Reel to reel. Deluxe TK 241." Bulky, heavy, but what a treat. I fought to keep my first and only tape recorder when the people in gray clothes came to get it, after the accident. And I did manage to, thanks to a spell of rage. There was some doubt about who it was who had brought the German-made tape recorder into the country ("introduced it," said the report they produced and goggled at with strong conviction). Mostly the investigators asked for the tape, as they had before the accident. Not *Missus Jones*. No, *Missus Jones*: "decadent, but it may pass." It was the other one they wanted, the tape Mother had supposedly brought home with the Grundig. It was inside, they insisted when she said she hadn't brought any tape home, and I suspected it wasn't a music tape they meant. There was a tape in the Grundig that Mother had not declared. Big and round, and illicit, they insisted. The dictionary definition of that word chilled me to the bone. It sounded like a word that could put my life in danger: "illicit."

"It was not my intention," she had said over the phone. That much I remember from one late summer afternoon shortly before the accident. She wore a cotton dress with a black floral pattern over a field of cobalt blue.

And:

"There was some mess" (no, that's not a word Mother would use), "there must have been some—misunderstanding. No. Yes, an unfortunate misunderstanding. At the airport, yes. The person I bought it from was in a hurry."

"No—a—friend. I mean, he was a friend's friend on business in our country. No, we don't have any. We don't have relatives abroad. Never had."

Then she laughed, "ha—ha—ha," in a low voice, unlike how she used to laugh on regular days, when she happened to laugh. Then she ran short of words or sounds. She grabbed a folded sheet of paper from the desk and fanned herself.

"I carried it myself. Straight home, yes. I mean—someone drove me home. A woman, an acquaintance from the hospital. They are reliable people, have worked for the government abroad. I ran into her at the airport and she offered to give me a lift.

"It's for my daughter. She's a teenager now and trains as a dancer, you see. That's why we need it. Two suitcases? I don't see what you mean. There must be some mistake, I'm afraid."

"Ha—ha—ha," she continued. "In any event, I had no time to touch it. I work, you know. It was just an occasion. A second-hand tape recorder, that's all. And—to tell the truth, we don't even know how to use it yet. Just three women in the house. You know, I have an old mother."

"Tell them we are honest people, Stela!" shouted Grandmother from the garden. "We don't want them in the house again. Tell them to stay away!"

She was trimming the rose bushes and making a lot of noise with the heavy scissors. I heard Stela shut the window, as if what

Grandmother said didn't matter, or maybe she just pretended she hadn't heard her.

A draft slammed the door. I stuck my ear to it. Held my breath.

"No—in the evenings I type. Articles for medical journals, translations. No, no texts of any other kind. Medicine is my field. I have a girl to raise, you see, an old mother."

"No, thank you. We aren't in need of anything. Thank you. We manage with what we have. We don't really need much, you know."

"But I do comply with the instructions, I do."

"To the office? To your office? Oh! Thank you! I am afraid, I—it's heavy, you see. In fact, had I known how heavy it was—Ah! Just the tape, you mean?"

She was running out of ha's. She coughed.

Then I felt something in Mother's tone that was not in tune with her manners. Another stream of syllables passed through the door instead:

"Someone, of course, can stop by and check what's on that tape, or even take it away."

Her voice dropped before she hung up. Then I heard her light step approaching the door. She must have rested her hand on the doorknob for a long moment, since I could hear her breath, and when it had slowed down, she came into the kitchen. Beyond suspicion, I was safely seated on my chair, busy molding bread-crumb manikins. She hadn't noticed me behind the living room door, and so much the better: there was enough embarrassment in the atmosphere already. I might have been dumb and clumsy, but at least I understood that much. Her face was the color of a whitewashed wall, the rims of her eyes thin red lines. I shrugged my shoulders. Could Mother fear anything? The bones of my thin legs suddenly felt as if they were made of cotton, my hands and fingers, too. Softly, a small white animal passed from Mother's shoulders onto mine, then under my skin. It nested in my stomach, or just a bit higher, in the place Stela called *the solar plexus*. The small white animal's heart throbbed with mine, or with a slight discord. Something told me Mother shouldn't hear how we'd bonded, the small animal and I, nor should she know how cotton feels when she held my hand. I raised my head and showed my pretty days smile. She held my head to her chest for a while, the combination of soap and moist warmth overwhelming.

"Shall we make that cherry pie, Miss?"

"Life takes over," that's what they say, the adults, right? "Wins," do they mean? "Succeeds?" Succeeds over what? And who were they to know how I managed? I wouldn't take advice from anyone.

Since my early years, Mother had warned me about minding who I talked to or whose steps I followed. She said I shouldn't trust strangers. But who else was there to trust? I kept my eyes wide open and complied with her instructions. She told me not to lie and I tried not to, no matter that the lines between what was really true and really false remained blurred. And, besides, I didn't have the slightest idea why there would be so much fuss about an old tape left (forgotten? introduced?) in a secondhand tape recorder. Unless it was as good as the one I listened to over and over, *so hush little baby, don't you cry!*

{6}

The Carpet

I walk up and down my burnt sienna carpet. When days are dark and the body is idle, I lie on it. I lie still on the burnt umber rectangle, flanked by two trees shaped like a fish's backbone (one yellow, the other blue) and three green camels. I breathe slowly and after a while my abdomen throbs, then my chest. Slowly, the panther escapes its cage, and all I have to do is watch my body keep up with the situation. I explore all its parts, one by one, drop them in the flat of my hand, feel their texture. I hold the body parts in my arms. Rock them. Then the panther slips back into its hideout and I go about my duties, not without a certain sense of commitment that helps me face the situation.

Day after day, I go on, carry out each movement properly, perform ordinary tasks as befits the circumstances.

On odd days, I dole out my little bones.

On even days, I string them all together on a thread.

Here I am, ambling on an empty sidewalk. Over there, on the other side of the street, my life is on the run. I smile and wave with no hard feelings.

In the absence of Stela, I have adjusted to that staggering rhythm.

> *Aye, my little bones*
> *Aye, aye, my faithful dog*

{7}

Waves

No matter what doubts I had about the accident, early on it became clear that I had to find a place for Stela, a place from where she would let me into her dreams, as I had let her into mine.

In her scarlet dress, her auburn hair framing her smooth complexion, she lies in a plush-lined gondola, comforted by the waves.

The fog drops over Venice, as it has time and again.

The waves grow more and more compelling, the breeze stronger. Gusts of wind and salt crack my lips. Bitter water goes down my throat.

Then her face begins to wear away. Water and salt.

Given a distinct pattern of space and atmosphere, a unique geometry of humors, I managed to restore Stela's smooth complexion, her uncompromising smile, her gift of healing. I wouldn't move, wouldn't utter a word. There was nothing else to do but stare at her.

My eyes would not accommodate a tear.

Over time, I could perform this trick whenever I wanted: bring Stela back, not because I missed her, it just gave me so much comfort to see how beautiful Mother still was. Had I told them, the others, about seeing Stela in her scarlet dress, comforted by the waves, they'd have pronounced me out of my mind. Some already considered that possibility in private. No, I never said a word about it. To gaze at Mother in her plush-lined hideaway was a gift given to me only. I had been tempted, yes, to expose my secret, to scare everyone around with it, to show how strong I was. But, then, did I really want to scare them away? Or did I want to be loved, by everyone, without fail?

{8}

Rewind

On the doorstep of the dilapidated barn I tilted and tottered with no intent. I straightened up. These awkward steps might be of use when I got back to dancing, lead me into new patterns. By degrees, my eyes adjusted to the damp darkness, from which a glittering array of metal popped up: the bent and crooked body parts of a car hanging from the beams, held by thin cords that were strong enough to bear that swaying weight. Wind passed through gaps in the walls with a slight tinkling sound, but I was already on my way out. Car debris was not something I felt like looking at, then or at any other time.

In the distance, horns blew at regular intervals: hunting horns, said someone in a tour group visiting the artists' village.

There was an agitation in the air. White undersides of gulls drifted above my head.

Atop a shabby wooden ladder splashed with white and red paint, a man coiled up wires strung in the branches of a wild apple tree.

A house—or what remained of it—standing before an orchard, invited me in. At the far end of a long vestibule, a door opened onto a small room, empty but for a fresco of anonymous, inverse silhouettes: missing tiles, phantom furniture, halos of picture frames. As I was about to leave that exposed intimacy, where one wall's peeling wallpaper met another's window, I noticed the flicker on the screen of a television monitor. Or was there more than one? Something slippery formed in the corner of my eye. Something that would not sustain words. I held my breath, stopped short. The videotapes hissed on and on. One monitor's image lagged slightly behind the other's. The screens were mostly colorless, clear, amniotic.

When her face drew closer and her lips were about to sketch an imperfect circle, a freeze-frame kept her from breathing her word. Then the movement continued, but inversely, backward, faster now, almost dashing. The woman's gestures, so fluid just a moment ago, fractured slowly before dissolving into a blur. The screen went black, and then white letters unfolded over the darkness—*part water, we serve beauty in the same fashion*—and when I almost blacked out, the cycle resumed. The lack of sound was less unsettling than the slightly wavering rhythm of the two duplicate tapes, their abrupt to and fro, in spite of which I was able to stand in front of Stela: firm, dependable, eager.

More than my seeing her again, what mattered was that Stela look at me.

{9}

Tunnels

With rigor and care, I accomplish my chart of steps devised for train journeys while guessing when exactly we have passed into a new country and what it feels like. Can I make out the divide? The precise spot where it occurs? Over the trees lining up in haste? Between the fields unfolding their versatile spectrum of colors? Or in the stretches of blue—of so many kinds—now a wide surface, now a strip sneaking among red rocks? This border is so unlike the ones Luca and I have crossed, our hearts racing, a knot throbbing in the throat, because there isn't any borderline. Times have changed; the borders we crossed before remained lines within our bodies, inner scars by which we can now measure the sweet confusion of not being able to tell where the frontier was. Curled up in my seat, alert, I look out the window, estimate my location as well as I can.

Small boats of many sun-fed shades synchronize their motions with the waves. White sails mimic the seagulls resting on the water. Suddenly a path, a flight of stairs climb toward nowhere, next, an abandoned train depot runs parallel with the new rails. On a quick road, a little man carries his thoughts. In no time, another drops his coat in the sand, behind the rocks.

A woman in a crimson blazer rushes to the lighthouse with a plastic bag in her arms. Behind the rocks, the man takes his nap. But this is another man. Two boys floating in tires on the water flap their skinny arms calling for a reply, or just hoping some traveler will carry the memory of their small bodies, their yearning smiles into farther spaces. A slim figure, a man with a backpack standing on a surfboard, paddles himself around on the flat sheet of water, like a hiker.

And there are houses now and then—light yellow, ochre, coral, and tall stone portals, a toy castle, a broken statue, a garden fountain guarded by four sirens cast in iron, a bronze swan, its back polished by so many kids who took a ride on it.

Five agile white swans perform their toilette in the grass. A woman gives her weight to the water, and I am eager to see what develops in the tunnels: what other pictures do these fugitive landscapes or their temporary inhabitants spark off, where will they carry me? There are so many tunnels, all of them unequal in length.

Are we in the other country yet? Perhaps the border passes as we run through the tunnel. In the rushing darkness, it occurs to me that I have brought Stela this far. As far as I could. All the way out. She is light, quite easy to lose track of. Like quicksilver, any minute now she could slip through a hole in my pocket, down the lining, and then, what else, down the road. I roll an amber bead between my fingers. *Ich geh' mit meiner Laterne.* One day, a trail of violet sequins will drift through my fingers, drop into the grass and I won't even know what that was. Then, *Rabimmel, rabammel, rabum—*

But I am vigilant in the extreme. I check on the items that carry Stela's imprint again and again, look for particular signs.

Fine cheekbones, high forehead, a rash on the face.

Stela's way of tilting her head. Her finely rounded shoulders, alabaster legs, her thin ankles.

Mutti folding clothes dried in the sun, smoothing them with the back of her hand, catching rainwater in a basin to rinse our hair.

Mutti dropping blood red cherries—wild, sour, sweet—into creamed butter, or spreading an interstice of ground walnuts between the pastry sheets, then apricot and rosehip jam, and a lace of meringue on the top for what she called "the Greta Garbo finish," a tip she had from her mother.

The turn of Stela's hand when she slips her arm into the sleeve of her raglan coat lined with moiré, or when she rubs some dark matter into some small box, then brushes her eyelashes with her lids half-closed, two small butterflies pulsating, by turns, at the end of each eye.

Mutti weaving coral baby rose branches into a wreath for her first-prize girl (once), telling the girl to straighten her back (more than once) and to always say *pardon* when she wants to make her way out of a crowd.

On their way to the dance class, little Cora urging her:

"Mutti, let's switch to the other language, play foreigners!"

German wasn't my mother's tongue, we aren't German, but Grandmother had us learn it, both Mother and I, as a reminder of where she came from—the Empire—a detail that was not to be mentioned at school. For at school, Grandmother had to be no one, an idea I didn't like but had to comply with. Being no one kept you out of danger. I somehow figured that out in spite of my convictions. Of course, my German was little more than approximate, but it felt good enough to speak it with Mother. Some words I just played by ear but she was able to make them out—I knew she would—it was a code between us that no one could break.

She takes Cora by her hand, whispers something, and down the street they go, Stela not quite touching the ground, not quite bending her knees or flexing her ankles, more like gliding down a moving walkway. Some people think we are sisters. Others, with vile gazes, conceal plots behind our backs. But Stela doesn't seem to care. I move past her, copycat her gait, and stumble once in a while.

I am only a sketch of her full figure, an approximation, more or less. Who isn't? Though I'd rather be more of her.

Hopscotch! say the chalk lines on the hot asphalt. Her fine ankles wobble in heels higher than she is in the habit of wearing, but she hops into each and every square like a baby bird not minding the sticky asphalt, as she used to when she was a child herself, not so long ago, it seems, from the ease of her steps. She plays hopscotch like a dancer on a net, or a buoy on a wave. Like chimney smoke. Or shingles. I don't know. She does it like only Stela would.

It happened long ago.
It happens every day.

The train stops. Someone's cell phone gurgles three times like a real phone. Billboards in another language stand above the wide open landscape, and a tiny old lady with short, freshly permed hair, asks me in a deep voice with slow, round vowels how far we are from the next stop. We are already there, at the next and last stop, and there's no one in view to check on us. I help the lady down the steps and leave her in the arms of two sunburnt grandsons, maybe the boys who, just a while ago, waved to the passing train from their round rubber vessels.

We have come to a warm country that feels like a home.

{10}

Setting

As instructed in the letter of acceptance, I have to be at the dancers' residence before dinner. There's time to take a walk, figure the place out, the endearing sadness of a border town, its puzzling seduction. Right in front of the train station, I am welcomed by what I had long anticipated: an arrangement of fir trees, umbrella cypresses, pines of all shades, and, at the end of the road, water. A lot of water: lilac, deep green, azure, shining gray, shimmering white, with its bouquet of salt, algae, fish. And the day's stage set is a narrow dam. Above, gulls display their repertory of wing beats. They draw circles with variable contours, more or less oval, that zigzag and turn into other shapes, shapes of an age-old pattern printed somewhere in the sky's tissue. Wherever they go they do that. There's reason in it. There's an urgency.

As I sit there under the searing sun, the idea visits me that there must be a way to get in touch with them. From where I am, I mostly see their chalk white undersides flickering in the dense sky like the dancing figures that keep moving behind my eyelids. And from that vantage point, it's hard to tell if there's joy or sadness in their flight, should that be a matter of concern. Still, what puzzles me is that I've come this far and still don't know. I do not know whether it's me who carried them along, perhaps farther than they ever wanted to go, or whether—with their flapping, whooshing, and squawking calls, their imperfect circles, lozenges, swaying Vs, and knots, which they keep doing and undoing—it was them who pushed me on.

I walk to the end of the dam. Sea salt has eaten up its edges from all sides. And perhaps because the water is so clear, I don't mind that. I don't mind the water's taste when the breeze spills it over the dam. I sniff the drops on my arms and lick the coating of salt they leave behind when they've dried. A sea swallow approaches me and seems to be picking something from my hair. They do that in Patagonia, I've heard, the land where I come from, Grandmother teased me because I was too tall for my age.

When I have seen enough water and breathed enough salt, it's time to go. The salt has tired me out. The flickers of the gulls have confused my eyesight. Suddenly, I feel exhausted, and I need to save my energy. Having come this far, about to meet my future fellows, I can't dash their expectations.

Deep green, plume-shaped cypresses flank the road to the mansion where I will spend some time working out my steps in good company.

At the end of the road, a lithe young lady greets me with a trustworthy smile. She seems so much part of a new plot I'm entering.

I drop the weight of material life in her hands and hurry to get ready to meet my new friends.

{11}

The Dream Solution

Just before I go to bed, it starts raining. The light changes from orange and pink to ostrich egg green, and large congregations of clouds linger before drifting toward unknown destinations. Then the festoon of hills vanishes under a thick white curtain. When small flickering lights scatter all over the hills, I unfold and latch together the bleached Mediterranean shutters. It rains all night and, in between one moment of sleep and another, I listen to the tempo of the rain's pattering on the roof.

A buzz wakes me up early and it's not only bees. I pull open the lower frame of the shutters and bend down to peer through the slats. Someone is busy mowing the lawn in a light so clear that it gives each blade of grass an expression of its own. Farther away, bales of hay welcome the sun, vine rows open down the hill into colossal fans. With a feline pace, I drag myself back to bed and indulge in a couple of quiet hours to work out my routines, eyes closed.

It is early but already hot. The day seems smooth beyond suspicion. Slowly, a torpor settles in, one that comes with the end of a long summer day rather than its beginning. And although it feels like the tamed alertness of sleep, I can still hear the morning's soundtrack in the garden, the mower humming, the bees buzzing. I can feel the sun drawing a warm tattoo on my face through the narrow slats. And I stay still for a while, suspended between the chattering outside and a smooth reviving breeze that comes from elsewhere.

Sometime between the mowing and the humming and the buzzing and the warm tattoo, it comes in one fell swoop—from the train platform to the bench in the Botanic Garden and beyond its tall gate—and I fear (I wish?) it will never stop. But time is short. Means of communication limited. She has done her best to look well, to stay unchanged. Stela wears a lime green trench coat in spite of the high temperature. I cannot hear her well. She draws circles with her hands, uses a pencil on a piece of worn-out paper. There had been a notebook, but she had to burn it late at night, in the backyard of our house. A ring was less conspicuous to leave behind. Someone kept calling to ask for a tape. The woman at the registration office had insisted on borrowing it. Stela couldn't say no. She had barely brought the second-hand tape recorder home and hadn't had time to listen to the tape, hadn't even noticed the Grundig had come with a tape under its heavy lid before the woman from the registration office, then some other well-meaning person, a police agent, mentioned that detail. (How did that woman know about the tape? She drove Stela home from the airport, yes, but when would she have raised the heavy lid to find out there was a tape in it? Unless she, or someone she knew, had slipped it inside, to compromise Stela or persuade her to compromise on her obsolete rules of honor and respect). Yes, there were other possibilities. Too many. Each with its lot of complications. But I had to be kept away from danger. Because accidents happened every day. And who would want to worry about an accident once it had happened and its traces had been erased for some, fabricated for others? Many vanished this way; Mother was in such bleak company. Most did not complain, took no action, no revenge. They did not believe in hate, or envy, or revenge. It helped them carry on, trusting—so far as trust would go—that the drift net they'd been caught in would not—could not—prevail. She had no evidence, no witness, no defense. And, after all, there wasn't any accusation against her, only innuendoes, or rumors at most. Then, suddenly, accidents she'd heard about happening to others started happening to her own family, too: one after another, one not necessarily related to the other (some did speak of fate, yes, while others remained frozen in silence). Stela had seen her father go to prison never to get out. She had to pay damage to the instigator of her father's car accident—or was the man just a doer, someone who obeyed? That road worker who'd thrown himself in front of the car had children to raise, a lawyer told her. (The doctor did, too. The doctor, who knew her from the hospital where she worked, took her out in the street with a casual sign of his hands and a nod of his head in the direction of the door, and they walked on the boulevard for a while, then took a narrow street, and when they'd reached a safe distance from the dispensary, he took her by the arm and whispered: "The man more than likely threw himself in front of your father's car according to the plot—your father's car was moving too slow for that road worker to be hurt. He's got no more than a few bruises, no broken leg, but I have kids to raise." The doctor stopped, put a hand on her shoulder and, looking somewhere far away, then down at her, said: "I had to write that medical report as ordered. I'm sorry for your father, but, you know, it's only six months of penitential labor. Unless he's willing to cooperate: he can buy some time, keep you out of worries.") After her father's chest was smashed by a wall that collapsed at the waterworks and his body was thrown into the prison graveyard, she had seen people in the house search for this and that, inquire about silks and cashmeres (where did she get them and in exchange for what?), inquire about the typewriter, about words she'd used in certain circumstances that she would have been better off not using (oh, yes, she did say this or that, it was written in the records). They inquired about the languages she'd learned and had me learn and to what end. She saw them sequestrate whatever was left to sequestrate and argued to keep the piano (worthless, out of tune, she insisted, who'd want a bulky piece of wood in their house?). But still, she was ready to help someone stuck in a remote place, whose life depended on a letter that had to reach a man of influence. And that's when she went away for some twenty weeks, yes she did, the letter lost in some gray car or seized by her abductors. But why would Mother go to the hospital for hepatitis, as she'd say on her return, when I knew, as she imagined I would, that as a doctor's assistant she could very well take care of herself? And why, then, would she break out of the hospital or whatever that was, as the rumor ran? At work, she did as well as she could with the contents of vials she had to inject into her patients or the pills she had to have them swallow. She had tried one out herself and half-experienced the effects she dreaded. She had slipped some of the vials into her pocket at the end of a long day, when she was in the office alone with her fear. She brought them home. Threw them in the gutters late at night. But new supplies of vials and patients arrived every other day. There was not much more she could do. She had a girl to take care of, an old mother. And where was her life going? She worked hard, eluded traps, kept to her secret rules, carried her smile along dark corridors. One hot summer morning she drove to the border river. Stood on the side of the road to get a glimpse of the world over there. Looked for clear water. But instead of clear blue water she saw bloated clothes floating on the turbid surface, or so it seemed to her tired eyes. A horde of rusted foreign-flag military vessels guarded the horizon. And she knew there was no place to go. She bent down and grabbed a handful of earth. Warm, crumbling. She tucked it into her pocket. She heard a rush of wind approaching, or was it a car, a slash? What happened next? She couldn't remember. The crack, she heard it. Yes, there was something like a crack, like an eggshell hitting the ground, and glaring chests, and huge wings of birds above, trimmed with white, silver, smoke. And streams of deep green water splashed from a hot-air balloon or something that had some such form. Briny drops rolled down her face, or what had been her face. Then everything turned into a cloudy, thick mass. And when she came to, a long, long time later, she was at the train station. She was there to provide some evidence, at last, of what she had seen in that remote place. Then something went wrong and it started all over again. A man she did not trust proposed a deal. And I was there. Someone must have said I should be. How couldn't I be there when Mother, who had been declared dead twenty years ago, was being returned by a government official? But she knew better. She did what she could to keep me out of it. Because what happened to her and everyone else matters little now. What matters is that I keep pace and balance on wooden planks with blistered paint. What matters is that *part water, we serve beauty in the same fashion because one's love is greater than oneself.* Because for each one who vanished, somewhere else another survived, deriving their strength from who knows what: a friend, a relative, the remains of sharing and trust, or, perhaps, from a tree's sudden blossom, a handful of syllables rehearsed in the dark, a capacity for wonder they'd managed to spare. She has other things to tell me. So many. But, without notice, we are running short of time; she says for now I have to focus on my opening, patch up whatever I can, and, yes, I should call her.

"Please. Do not forget to call, Miss."

"I will, Mutti, you can count on me."

And I look for coins in my pocket. Instead of small change, there's a dark red amber bead lingering in there, smooth, almost round. Then shadow and light rotate, and a sudden eclipse transforms the leaves of an ailanthus tree standing alone in the open field into bright goldenrod half-moons, before they are no more than a peaceful breath in the dark. The bead drifts through my fingers, drops in the grass, and rolls there for a while before I lose sight of it. Had I bent down and touched it, it might have broken.

By eight I pull out my notebook with a drowsy hand, grope for a pen and write it all down: inklings, suspicions, conjectures, one reversing the other, one an ally to the other. My hand hurries to record them in one go, as they came, in the order they came. When I have written down what I remembered of Stela's return and what I could make out about her disappearance, I pull the bed sheet to my chin and see my heart throb under that white cotton skin. Something warm lingers on my chest. Outside, the bees are still revolving in jazzy patterns and I know it's time for me to get up.

A shooting pain slows my right wrist. And where I have held my head in my left hand as I was writing, a crease has formed, like a slash. I look in the mirror at the wrinkles printed on my face and smooth them out as well as I can with my fingers. But I don't really mind the wrinkles. They are Mutti's and Maia's, surfacing in translucent layers over my face in the mirror, and when I'm out on the paint-blistered wooden boards, they'll shine in the summer night. I walk to the window to see how far the mowing machine has moved and if the company is up. I stretch my body, wash my face, brush my teeth, pass my fingers through my hair, tie it into a ponytail, then let it loose. Now I'm ready to start my day, to do my workout for the opening night: bend, stretch, leap, and unreel all I have seen, get the misty figure in the dream to move along with me, then set Stela free from the circling doubts that have held us back for twenty years.

Of course I think of Luca and how the script will read once I've deciphered my shorthand of the dream, expanded its possibilities, joined them to the alternatives we had explored and, eventually, exhausted. Didn't he intimate once, when we walked in the fields rimmed with poppies, that he might take Stela's video portrait farther? Into a larger picture? Why had our paths crossed again? But for now, on my way to the company's improvised studio, I just scribble a word to him on the back of a postcard I've kept in my notebook with a drawing he loved: a cat—"very pale at the shoulders," the caption says—patting a dog with a plume in his mouth:

You were right about brain spots—pictures—partial solutions
further processing in progress   the connecting machine about
to be fixed
you are a genius
I think I love you (if I may)

P.S. sometimes, the imagination's is the only room there is

{12}

The Opening Night

Or so they called it, although it was to be, according to the company's habit, a one-time event.

When I joined them, I had to start from scratch, as advised by the Dance Maestro. "You always have to," he said. "Forget, or almost, what you've been trying out for years, day after day. Don't think of the body's limits but of how you can befriend them. Forget about nice moves. Just make it right. Persist. You'll know it when it has come. Reach the bone, you can do that, and, remember, the brain too has its ways of recovering," he says, "just like a muscle. Take all weight out of your way till the body you carry on your shoulders—here, right here—is no more than light fabric, water flowing, streams of water and light."

"He's right," whispers someone by the wooden rail, her head upside down, "lack of tension will support you—in the most extra-or-di-na-ry way."

"And you'd better watch your ankles," carries on the Maestro. Ankle for one, wrist for the other; shoulder, thigh, torso, he will catch the weak point in every one of us, have the right word for each. For me, he'd leave a book wrapped in a grocery bag every other day on the windowsill of my tiny room. And if I rarely had the time to read, at night, when my bones rested, it only mattered that someone cared. In just a few months, he'd helped me reach what had failed me, find out how to arrange whatever gestures came my way, above all, tame my breath.

Throughout the summer we've had time to practice our steps, our comings and goings, have our moves join together. Time to refine our provisional arrangements, the varied qualities of motion, the clarity of our project's intent. Now the season is drawing to its end: hot humid days, reviving cobalt blue nights. Cypresses and parasol pines watch over our busy bodies, night drops a slow curtain where our stage has none, glowing dragonflies liven it up. White and violet and green lights pulsate in the distance, a sea of minute lanterns we look at for direction, and we know the time has come for us to set the performance off.

A platform has been cantilevered out over the hillside for the occasion, washed with the lavish southern sun, a platform with which we have to make do, provided it holds, later, on the lip of the night. As we practiced in the mid-summer heat, I had imagined it as a turning stage, with painted sets, colored beams holding the body, auras projecting in the dark. But, look, that's all there is: just a platform improvised for the event.

Yet no one seems to mind. We are each other's company and the blue-green night that embraces the platform is better than any handmade set. We all stand still, preserve our energy, rehearse the steps behind our lids, perform our secret rituals. I, for one, recite Luca's dictum: "Don't stare at your arm but at the space it's meant to reach."

Luca will be missing from the audience. He can't make it, but he sent a letter the Maestro slid under my door this very morning. And it is just as well with me. He will, yes, he'll think of me, catch and change trains tomorrow in the early morning, then find a car to get here. It's a long way from north to south, he knows, but he'll join me before long. He has unplugged the monitors, left them in the room where they've spent a year that revived the village with the artists' works made for the occasion, took only the videotape that we have found a title for: *Stela*. He packed, dropped the amber beads I left behind in a handkerchief, tucked it in his pocket, then met his friends at *De Blauwe Grens* for one last drink. Tomorrow, the village will be forsaken yet again. Visitors, team-workers, artists, will all go their way. Some will, perhaps, recall a broken wall, others a fleeting image, some a voice in a garden, a draft in a barn, others not much. He hopes his letter reaches me in time. And just in case it didn't (this is Luca), a telegram arrived this morning, too: *The lost keeps the found in equipoise.* For once the mail brings in comforting news.

Accidents happened in the early evening. "Ominous," I feared. "Just part of it!" the Maestro declared to reassure us all. A storm whose signs had remained unnoticed by the weather forecast stirred up the branches. The electricity went out. A light pole collapsed on the stage, bulbs burst spilling tiny slivers of glass on the rough wooden planks, a menace to our soles, but that was no disaster.

Then the wind died away, light was restored, and we were ready to go.

I step on the planks and follow the fabric of the colored beams. And if I cannot see the shapes my body draws within the lattice of the lights, I do catch sight of the other dancers stretching, flexing, leaning, and pulling, shuffling, falling, and rising. Their bodies' signs tell me where I am. The floor throbs under their steps and I move with its heartbeats. Waves of breath, drops of sweat pass by me in haste. I hear my companions trace imperfect circles, beat and ripple the air. I hear them trace straight and broken lines, feel them cross, brush one another's shoulders, then pull apart. When I withdraw, they perch, and lope, and twist, they stumble or clash, meet with discord, look for resolution. Stop—run. Stop—hold. Enter—exit. There is a rhythm to it. There is a reason.

When they have all dissolved into the dark, in the wings improvised for the occasion, I look up, put my right hand on my chest to slow down my racing heartbeat, fix my gaze on a small lantern in the distance, then step out on the plank floor.

My turn has come.

My solo.

I dance as if someone's life was at stake tonight.

It's all I can do.

My leotards are the color of skin and the lighting cues transform them through so many complexions, my hair loose, as it's meant to be: part of the body, part of the dance. I spin and fall and rise, I do small leaps across the stage, then stop, count my breath, and when I've stood still as long as I can manage, a soft-paced man steps out of the dark, drops a fluttering silver tunic on my shoulders. When I stretch out my arms, I wear iridescent wings, like an insect's. I fold and unfurl them as best I can. The wind rises once more, precipitates confusion. A blurred form takes hold of my steps. A shade uncoils. I hear a step within and I stand still to keep the restless flame close to my chest, then see it flare, flow down my arms, slip through my fingers, rise, and hesitate before the sleepy figure dwelling in my body moves out of sleep.

Then I let go.

Above my head, the silver fabric lingers for a while before it drifts in the direction of the audience, testing layers of air, changing shades, and shimmering as it levitates in the night. This is the moment when my torso revolves around an invisible axis, the moment when a thin luminous column twists into a spiral. It turns while I rotate. And what that spiral holds remains still.

No solid body is lighter than air

The wind has left behind a steady drizzle that gains momentum as I move. Raindrops drip down my body, change its temperature, its consistency. Then the drops dry up, leave a film of briny crystals on my shoulders.

The music, the wind have broken off. Stirred by the full moon, cicadas take over, cypresses spread their breath across the hills.

I bow, salute the audience, the companion with myriad eyes they've been for a while—perhaps the only one—and even Luca may, after all, be hiding out there. He alone would see that tonight I gave Stela, and myself, another life. A flight of unoffending feet joins me from the wings. Our damp palms circulate a moment's accord, ignoring the exhaustion that steams up in the dark. Persistence and luck have brought us farther into the body's limits, farther than we've ever thought we'd go—each ignoring the others' future destinations even while we shared the warmth of our skin for the time of a dance. And wherever our steps have meant to rush us, what else have we found than how to cope with what's at hand and, mostly, with what is not?

The night smells of burnt cloth.
It smells of soap, clear water, milk.

Acknowledgments

Portions of this work have appeared in somewhat different form in *Absinthe: New European Writing* and online at *FREQUENTLYNOWHERE*. The author gratefully acknowledges the editors of these publications.